I0535132

THE CLIFFS OF DEATH

THE CLIFFS OF DEATH

CLAUDETTE NICOLE

CUTTING EDGE

Copyright © 1968 Claudette Nicole

The characters and events portrayed in this book are fictitious. Any similarity
to real persons, living or dead, is coincidental and not intended by the author.
No part of this book may be reproduced, or stored in a retrieval system, or
transmitted in any form or by any means, electronic, mechanical, photocopying,
recording, or otherwise, without express written permission of the publisher.

ISBN-13: 978-1-970848-10-6

Published by
Cutting Edge Books
PO Box 8212
Calabasas, CA 91372
www.cuttingedgebooks.com

CHAPTER ONE

The girl hurried down the deserted road, her long, lithe figure bent slightly forward, her black hair streaming loosely behind her. She had wakened early after having slept surprisingly well, and she had promised herself she wouldn't think about the letters. She wouldn't think about them or do anything impulsive about them. She pulled the trench coat tighter around her gray-green sweater and gray slacks, glad she'd remembered how chill the early dawn could be. And now she had reached the beach of firm white sand, gently curving.

Slowly she walked alongside the sea. The breakers shattered thunderously, sending salt spray flying against her face, and the sea birds swooped low over her, seeming to want a closer look at the stranger on their beach. Over everything was the grayness, the unrelieved, unbroken grayness of early dawn on the Irish coast. The grayness and the wind's bite were as much a part of the Connemara coast as the peat bogs were a part of Ireland. The North Atlantic swept the wind in as a morning song, wild and bleak and beautiful, but with it all a soft mistiness, a promise of something better to come. It was as if God had never been able to decide whether to make this a harsh or a gentle place.

It is the same, the girl whispered to herself, *the very same.* And suddenly she was terribly glad for the constancy of things that never change. A wry smile escaped her as she thought how little she had once valued constancy. She paused to kick off her shoes and press her toes into the firm sand. As she neared the cluster of rocks that jutted out almost to the water's edge, she wondered whether he would be there. She paused as she reached the first of the stones. Would he? she asked herself again as she carefully made her way around the narrow space at the end of the rocks. She felt her steps quicken, and she pulled herself back. How utterly ridiculous, she told herself. Old habits certainly do die hard. But then, it really hadn't been that long. Or had it? Is long ago measured in days or weeks or years? Or is it really measured in the things which leave their mark, those unforgettable things which happen to us? She turned the edge of the rocks and saw the figure sitting there. She was annoyed at how her heart leaped. Once again she had to stop herself from running forward, clambering up the rocks. With deliberate slowness she stepped onto the rocks, aware of his eyes watching her. He was the same, too, she saw happily, the same dark, unruly hair, the dark blue eyes that spoke a language of their own.

Time and the years had etched a few new lines on the rugged head, but they only added a new strength. Now she was beside him, and her eyes met his, levelly. She eased herself down upon the flat rock, surprised at how like yesterday it seemed.

"Brian," she said softly.

His eyes looked out to sea, searching the grayness. Finally he spoke, not looking at her.

"I wondered if you'd come," he said slowly, his voice still rich and deep, overlaid with the soft velvet of the coastal tongue.

"Of course," she said.

"I'm glad," he answered, his eyes still focused on the sea. "I'm glad for her sake. She would have wanted you at the funeral; you more than anyone else."

"I know," the girl said. She didn't want to talk of her aunt's funeral, or of the fear inside her. Not now, not this moment.

"Brian," she said, surprised to hear the hesitancy in her voice, "how are you?"

Now he turned and looked down at her, his eyes traveling across her face, examining the milk-white skin, the shoulder-length black hair and the light blue of her eyes. Silently, she hoped time had treated her as kindly as it had him.

"Welcome back to Duncavan, Sheila McCloud," he finally said, unsmiling.

"Thank you," she answered. "I arrived late last night. I'd wired Terence to have my room ready, and I went right to bed. But I had to come down here this morning. It was the very first thing I had to do, somehow."

He didn't reply. His eyes just watched her.

"Do you still come here every morning?" she asked. "Or was this just a coincidence?"

"I still come every morning," he said quietly.

"I'm glad," Sheila commented.

"Why?"

Was there a touch of bitter amusement in his eyes?

"I don't know why," she answered honestly. "I just am, somehow."

Sheila clasped her hands around one knee and leaned forward. The wind swept her hair to one side as she looked sideways up at the serious, unsmiling man beside her. Yes, he was the same, too; the same quiet, comforting strength, the same steadiness that made just being with him a reassuring experience. It was there, unmistakably there—as if there had never been those years, and somehow, once again, she was glad, unexplainably glad.

"I feel as though I'd never left," she breathed.

"But you did," he said, and she was grateful for the gentleness in his voice. "And now the funeral has brought you back."

"Not just the funeral," Sheila said, and saw his eyebrows raise in silent question. She shook away thoughts of the letters and the cold fear that instantly leaped up inside her.

"I don't want to talk about it, not this first morning back in Duncavan," Sheila said, impulsively reaching out to touch his jacket sleeve. "I just came here because this is where we used to talk without talking, where we'd draw strength from the sea and the wind and just being together. "I'm glad you were here, Brian. I wanted it to be the same as it used to be. Good old Connemara sentimentality, I guess."

"Only the same is never the same," Brian said. "Even when it seems to be, it really isn't. That sand you walked on isn't the same sand you used to walk on. The sea has turned it over a hundred times. That rock you sit on isn't the same rock you left. It's been burned by a thousand suns and battered by a million waves. It only looks the same."

"But it's still there," Sheila answered quietly.

"Aye," he admitted, "that's true enough. It's still there."

The grayness was beginning to lighten now, and the wind to lose its bite as the sun fought its daily struggle to break through. Brian pushed himself to his feet, held his hand out to Sheila and effortlessly pulled her up beside him. She always felt so small next to Brian. He wasn't that tall, but there was something sturdy and rugged about him that made her feel tiny. And now, for the first time, he smiled down at her, and there was a warmth in his eyes which could reach down and gather her up like an eager kitten.

"I've got to be starting back, Sheila McCloud," he said. "I do work for a living, you know. Come now; let's go."

She fell into step beside him, pausing to retrieve her shoes where she'd left them. They walked slowly, as they used to do, and she fought down the desire to take his arm. She glanced up at the lined face, the creased forehead and full lips and the rock-like strength of it. His face was so like this land, strong and lined, yet soft and tender withal. It was little wonder she'd never been able to forget him. God knows she had tried hard enough. But it had never really worked. She thought of that lovely line from *Galway Bay;* she might as well have "tried to light a penny candle from a star." It couldn't be done. And now she was back here in Duncavan, older, a little wiser, she hoped, and even more unsettled and frightened than that day she'd left seven years ago.

"Brian," she said, "I do want to talk to you as soon as possible. When can I see you officially? Are you still the only lawyer and real estate agent in Duncavan?"

"Solicitor," he reminded her. "You're not in America now. It's solicitor here."

"Of course." She laughed. "I'd forgotten. You're handling Aunt Margaret's affairs, aren't you?"

"As much as she let anybody handle them," Brian answered. "You'll be staying for the reading of the will, I expect. I'll try to hurry that, but it may take a bit of doing."

"How do you mean?"

"Well, everything happened so suddenly, the accident was so unexpected, that there's been not time to find the will yet. It's among her things somewhere, I'd imagine."

"Why isn't it filed with you, in your office?" Sheila asked in surprise.

"That's easy to answer. Because your aunt didn't want it that way. You know how she was. All she had me do was add my signature as a witness. She said she wanted nobody knowing her thoughts until it was too late for them to argue with her, and that included me."

That would be Aunt Margaret, all right, Sheila knew, and suddenly the dread and guilt and anger filled her thoughts again.

It must have shown on her face, for she saw Brian was looking at her sharply.

"What is it, Sheila?"

"Nothing … nothing."

"Don't tell me that, lass," he said. It always had been impossible to lie to him.

"All right; I am disturbed … very disturbed," Sheila said. "And I do want to talk to you, but I want a little more time first."

"Sounds mysterious," he commented. "You've picked up a touch of the dramatic in New York, I see. How about tonight … dinner? I'll pick you up at seven."

"That would be wonderful," Sheila said, brightening. It would give her time to talk to Terence. They had reached the fork in the road from the beach where a small *carn*, a cluster of stones, marked the two converging roads. Brian would be taking the one that led into Duncavan.

"Tonight, then," he said as he turned quickly and walked off. She watched his figure go down the road until the morning mists closed him off. She was watching him just as she used to do every morning. She was thoroughly annoyed at herself for the way she felt. She hadn't expected to feel this way at all. She hadn't even planned to visit Duncavan until her aunt's last two letters. Or had she? Sheila mused as she walked up the road. She recalled how, on a recent night, she'd looked from her window at the mists in Central Park and seen the mists of Mara Valley. At a florist on Lexington avenue, she had stood staring at some violet flowers, seeing the fuchsia that bordered the lough in the valley. Maybe coming back had been closer to her real desire that she'd let herself know. But it had been Aunt Margaret's death that had made the trip immediate, and now she had to gather her own thoughts, to make her own plans. First she wanted to talk to Terence, then spend the rest of the day in town.

She found the road up to where the great manor house tow-ered majestically was longer than she'd remembered. She was out of breath when she stood at the door of Doylan Hall, letting the iron knocker fall against its hammered plate. When Terence opened the door, the old man's eyes widened.

"Miss Sheila! I thought you were upstairs asleep."

"I know." Sheila laughed. "I went for an early walk on the beach."

She flung her coat onto a high-backed chair in the wide entrance hall and linked arms with Terence. His hair was a bit whiter, the step a bit slower, but the crinkly smile was an echo of her childhood.

"How long has it been, Terence?" Sheila asked. "I can't remember Doylan Hall without you."

"I can't recall exactly any more, Miss Sheila," the old man said, a sadness coming into his eyes. "Forty … fifty years … I don't think on it. You don't think about how long you've been happy. It's the unhappy ones who count the days, who know exactly how long they've been doing something or been some place. No, all I count these days are my pipes."

"Your pipes!" Sheila exclaimed, clapping her hands impulsively. "Are you still collecting? You must have scads of them by now."

The old man's eyes brightened, and with a happy chuckle he beckoned her to follow as he shuffled to the door of his room. The room was as she had last seen it, the small desk to one side, the leather chair, deep-seated and comfortable, the old brass lamp and the walls lined with glass-covered cedar cases. But now there were many more cases, and she knew Terence was alive with happy pride as she marveled and gasped and enthused about each one.

"And of them all, ye know what my favorite still is, don't you now?" Terence said, reaching into the side drawer of the little desk to bring out a glistening, deep-bowled pipe.

"Of course," Sheila exclaimed, "the meerschaum." It had been given Terence by her aunt and had belonged to Thomas Moore.

"This above all," Terence said, carefully putting it back in the far reaches of the drawer. "I like to smoke it more than all the rest put together. It makes its own kind of pipe dreams for me, Miss Sheila."

"I'm hungry, Terence," Sheila announced. "Does that sound familiar?"

"It does that … familiar and grand to hear in this house again. We've a new cook, Bridgit O'Rourke; only been with us four years."

Sheila smiled inwardly. Only four years. In terms of Doylan Hall, that would be a new cook, of course.

"I'll tell her you're waiting breakfast, Miss Sheila," Terence added.

"I'll wait in the drawing room," Sheila said. "And, Terence, a set of keys, please. That way I'll not be bothering you every time I go in and out."

Sheila turned and walked to the great drawing room of Doylan Hall. At the threshold she halted, shutting her eyes at the rush of scenes that tumbled down upon her: scenes of herself, a little raven-haired girl playing in the huge room; of her uncle, dimly remembered, and then only her aunt; scenes of a little girl growing up, studying in the huge chairs, curled up before the great fireplace; scenes of a multitude of wonderful Christmases, of the holly-decked mantelpiece and huge candles in heavy silver candelabra; of the delicate crèche that covered the window seats at Easter; of springtime and Aunt Margaret making every corner erupt in a cascade of flowers; scenes of uncounted, carefree years of utter happiness. Sheila opened her eyes and walked into the room. She had shared only twenty of the two hundred years of comfort this great room had given, but the heavy paneled wood-work instantly embraced her with sturdy security. The two tapestries hung from ceiling to floor on each side wall; the heavy sofa made a half-circle before the fireplace that took up the entire north wall.

Sheila halted before the fireplace and looked up at the full-length portrait of the regal-looking woman in a long white satin gown, her face sternly imposing but the flash in the blue eyes betraying the kindness and humor that lay behind her serious façade.

This was the woman who had raised her after her parents' death in a train accident, the woman who had given her not just home and comforts but strength, character, backbone and love, the kind of love that only the very wise and good can give. And now a tragic end had come to Lady Margaret Doylan, mistress of Doylan Hall, a fall from the edge of the fogbound cliffs onto the rocks and sea below. Instantly Sheila felt her lips tighten as cold apprehension flowed over her again, the unrealized alarm she knew had to be realized. Angry determination quickly following, she turned and walked briskly into the dining hall, where Terence had just brought in breakfast: muffins, sausages, jam and a huge kettle of tea. She sat down, feeling very small in the high-backed chair at one end of the long, glistening table, at one end of a table made for thirty diners.

"Terence," Sheila began as the old man poured the tea, "tell me about it. You were the one who found her."

She saw the old man's hand tighten on the handle of the kettle.

"Yes, Miss Sheila," he said. "I found her. When she didn't come down for breakfast and wasn't in her room, I got worried. When she didn't appear at all during the morning, I went looking for her. I walked up the moors to the cliffs. You know she used to love to sit there and look out to Inishshark. But she wasn't there. I don't know what made me look down. I don't like to look down. And there she was...."

Terence's voice trailed off, his lips working, with no sound coming from them, his shoulders shuddering. He pressed a hand against his forehead.

"I'm sorry to make you relive it again," Sheila said, "but there are some things I must find out. Why did you become worried when Aunt Margaret didn't come down for breakfast? Surely there have been lots of mornings when she either went out early or slept late. What else is there, Terence? I know there's more. What else do you know?"

"More, Miss Sheila? I don't know anything more." Terence answered quickly, too quickly. Sheila saw something flicker in his eyes, something made up of fear and uncertainty.

"There is more, Terence," she pressed. "Aunt Margaret always confided in you. You were in her complete trust. I want you to tell me everything you know. You know her death was no accident."

"Don't talk like that, Miss Sheila," Terence cried, backing away, his hand holding the tray shaking so that the dishes fairly leaped about. Now the agitation and fear in his eyes were undisguised. "It was an accident. It's over and done with now. There'll be no bringing her back."

Sheila watched him start to turn away.

"I've work to do, Miss Sheila," he said. "There's nothing more. Let what's done stay done."

The last was a plea, and he cast the girl a look almost of desperation. Sheila turned to her breakfast. Obviously there was more, and Terence was afraid. The letters tucked in her purse in her room rushed back at her. Terence's agitation gave them new substance. But why was he afraid to talk to her? Terence could be very protective, she knew. Was he trying to protect Aunt Margaret's memory from something that could tarnish or ruin it? If so, what could possibly do that? Or was he afraid for himself … for someone else? Let what's done stay done, he had pleaded. Perhaps it was just an old man's plea for peace. Perhaps there had been trouble, and now it would be ended. She knew Aunt Margaret had often tangled with townsfolk, other landowners, officials and just about anyone whose interests clashed with those of Doylan Hall. But no, there was more to it than just that. She felt it in her bones. And she would get at the truth, somehow. She would talk to Brian about it tonight. Meanwhile, she would go to town and see what a casual stroll through Duncavan might reveal.

CHAPTER TWO

The village of Duncavan lay on a narrow strip of flatland, a *curragh*, between the sea cliffs on the left and the valley to the right. The houses, mostly white, some a very pale blue tint, contrasting with the dark wood eaves and sloping thatched roofs, stood in neat rows behind low stone walls. There was the timelessness of a living fairy tale about this land, as though yesterday had never really gone and today had not really arrived.

As she neared the village, Sheila wondered what her reception would be like. Seven years ago when she'd left Duncavan for America, feelings had been running high, some for her and some against her. Brian and she had posted the banns, the wedding day had been set, and the whole town was emotionally involved. Not that it took much to accomplish that. The marriage of the niece of the mistress of Doylan Hall and the promising young solicitor would have been a social event in Galway. In Duncavan it had assumed the air of a major festival. Then came the bitter quarrels with Brian, the sudden shattering of a rainbow. Yes, she recalled, feeling had run high indeed, and she knew she'd not be far into Duncavan before word of her presence would be running like the blown milkweed ahead of her.

The first of the houses would be Tom Grogan's, standing at the corner of the main road leading through the village. When she reached the neat house, she saw the long ladder with Tom Grogan atop it, looking just the same, with, she'd have sworn, the same pair of patched overalls. He was busily rethatching his roof, she saw, spreading the marl, the soft yellow clay on which he would lay the new straw.

"May your new roof bring you new blessings, Tom Grogan," Sheila called out. The man turned, his eyes widening. He half leaped from the ladder.

"Sheila McCloud!" he shouted. "Am I seeing things, or is it really you?"

"It's me, all right," Sheila said, laughing. "In person, and glad to see you looking just the same, Tom."

"Well, you're a sight for sore eyes, Sheila McCloud," the man said. "Welcome back, lass. Welcome back." He turned and lifted his voice. "Agnes … Agnes, do you hear me? Come out and see who's here, woman."

Sheila had always liked the Grogans very much, Tom and his plumpish, good-natured wife, Agnes; and now her old fondness returned with a rush of overwhelming gratitude. It was heartening to have the first greeting such a warm and friendly one. Agnes appeared, wiping hands on apron, and rushed over with a crushing embrace.

"Oh, it's good to see you, Sheila," she exclaimed. "And don't you look smart, and even more beautiful than ever. But what a terrible thing to bring you back to us."

"Don't cut the ale, Agnes."

It was Tom Grogan interrupting, and Sheila smiled. It had been a long time since she'd heard that expression, and she turned it over in her mind as one turns over the memory of old friends suddenly remembered. Don't cut the ale … don't weaken a moment of happiness. Yet the reason for her return was always upon her. It couldn't really be put aside. She talked a few minutes longer with the Grogans and then walked on, passing Brannigan's Sweet Shoppe, Malachy's Tobacco Store and the local pub, The Whistling Dog. She could almost hear the hurried phone calls that followed her path and the whispered conversations. Now there were more people emerging from houses and stores to greet her. There were those who rushed over, filled with genuine joy and the native curiosity of the Irish dispelling the kind of warmth and friendliness she had felt with the Grogans. And there were those who nodded quietly and said a few polite words, while their eyes were filled with reserved interest. And there were some who met her glance and turned away. They, most of all, reminded Sheila of the deeply held attitudes of the connemara people, attitudes that, once adopted, formed themselves into immutable molds. It was a characteristic of the people that could be both a good and a bad thing. It helped make this land what it was, and what it wasn't. But Sheila was happy to note that the smiles far outnumbered the frowns, the greetings were more numerous than the silences. And then, in quick succession, she had two meetings which flooded her with sadness, wonder and fear. The first was with Marla Culchane. They almost collided physically as Marla came out of Treadwell's General store, grocery bags in her arms. Sheila's reaction was open, spontaneous.

"Marla!" she cried happily. When she saw the expression in the other girl's eyes, Sheila's mind leapt back across the years in a kind of instant playback. Marla and she had been girlhood friends until Brian came into the picture. The contest for Brian had never been open, never overt, until Brian and she had grown closer. Then Marla clearly became a rival. But the rivalry was short-lived, for Brian chose Sheila. So, in Marla's eyes, Sheila had won. Marla had been vicious, then hateful and spiteful. Sheila recalled how Marla had cornered her once at a dance and told her she was neither good enough nor woman enough for Brian and that she had won only because of her position and prospects as niece of the mistress of Doylan Hall. These things leaped up in Sheila's memory as she saw the look in Marla Culchane's eyes, a look made up of surprise, fright and venom. But she had to go on with it, or try, anyway.

"How wonderful to see you, again, Marla," Sheila said. "On my first day back, too."

"You've turned up again," the girl said through tight lips, "like a bad penny."

"You look very well, Marla," Sheila tried again, ignoring the girl's remark. Marla Culchane was indeed still a very attractive girl; a little heavier perhaps, but her auburn hair still glistened, and her face was smooth and unlined. It was the bitterness in her face that detracted from her prettiness.

"Marla," Sheila started over, "please don't feel that way. I don't harbor any old grudges or anything like that."

Marla Culchane's eyes flashed at her in anger.

"No, of course not," she bit out. "All you do is come waltzing back and think you can take charge again. Well, you won't, do you understand?"

Marla's face was clouded with hate as she leaned forward, the groceries in her arms trembling along with her body.

"You won't do it twice to me in one lifetime, Sheila McCloud," she half-screamed. "You'll get out of here if you know what's good for you. Today! Now! Go away and stay away!"

The girl strode off down the street, even her back reflecting hatred and fury. Sheila stood quietly, shaken, until she could gather herself. She forced herself to put aside the incident and walked on, stopping to chat with the Mulcahys and the Robinsons. She had just about reached the end of Duncavan when the second incident occurred. She had started to turn back when a small Austin Mini-van came to a halt across the street from her. A tall man, black-eyed, with unruly black hair with a strong jaw, a kind of handsomeness to him, got out and went to the rear of the little truck to unload some boxes. When he saw the girl, he stopped, a frown darkening his face, and Sheila saw the black eyes bore into her with a dark fire, an unconcealed hatred. She knew his face, and she searched her memory for something to bring his name to mind. Had he worked for Aunt Margaret? Yes, that was it, Sheila recalled. He had been hired as a gamekeeper on the hundred acres of land her aunt had kept as a game preserve across the valley. And now, as she recalled the man as he had come to apply for the job that first day, his name returned ... Bayliss, Robert Bayliss.

"Hello," Sheila said pleasantly, trying to see behind the burning expression his eyes.

"It won't make any difference," he said, growling the words at her.

"What won't make any difference?" Sheila asked.

"Your coming back, that's what," Bayliss answered. "If you've any brains at all, you'll get out of here as fast as you can."

He tossed the boxes into a yard, hopped into the little truck and sent it roaring off with a spray of dust and gravel that stung her legs. The unconcealed hatred of the man's eyes stayed with her as she started back through the village again. There were two people, at least, who had shown they were more than a little displeased at her return to Duncavan. Why were their feelings so much deeper than anyone else's? What did the man Bayliss have inside him to bring out such hatred? In the case of Marla Culchane, she could halfway understand old enmities still rankling, but not like this, not after seven years, not with the kind of venom she had spit out. There must be something more, something she was totally unaware of. As she passed the road leading off the right to where Brian's office was, she paused and hesitated. Then she went on. She'd ask about Bayliss at dinner that night, and about Marla Culchane. Had Brian been seeing Marla? she wondered. That might explain a lot about Marla's attitude. At

Dorrit Lane she spied the small, neat sign peering over the hedge: Constabulary. She wondered if Constable Connaughten was still there. Plenty of time to find out about that, too, later, she decided as she hurried on.

She walked slowly back to Doylan Hall and stood before its great gray stone walls, fingering the keys Terence had given her in the pocket of her jacket. She turned from the door of the house and began to walk diagonally across the lawn. Her path took her past the stables that were now garages and out toward the moors that stretched beyond the house, reaching to the cliffs that faced the sea. When she reached a point opposite the end of the Manor House, Sheila closed her eyes and began to walk with deliberate slowness. Step by step, keeping to a straight line, she held her eyes tightly shut. And then, suddenly, she felt the first puff of the wind. She slowed her pace even more, stepping tentatively. Eyes shut, she moved forward, and now she felt the wind grow stronger, felt it strike her face and swirl her hair. She halted and turned to the right and began to move in a slow curve, carefully, slowly, testing each step. Now she was talking aloud to herself. *There's a crag that bulges in ... about twenty feet. It can fool you. I can hear the sea now. After the bulge it cuts out and continues around.* Sheila felt the palms of her hands grow wet, and a little bead of perspiration trickled down her face. And then, suddenly, she felt her hair whipped around behind her to blow in the other direction. She stopped and opened her eyes. She was standing midway on the curve of the cliffs, not more than four feet from the edge.

"There! I knew it!" she announced to the wind. Seven years and she had still remembered. Seven years had not erased the imprint of a girlhood spent on these moors, walking these cliffs. Her certainty growing more certain with every passing minute, Sheila hurried back to Doylan Hall and let herself in. She heard Terence's voice from the kitchen. He was peeling onions and talking to a wide, pleasant-faced woman of about fifty, clothed in a white uniform. She turned and dipped in what Sheila realized was something remotely approximating a curtsy.

"This must be Bridgit." Sheila smiled. "I just stopped in to tell you I won't be here for dinner tonight. I'm going out for the evening with Mr. O'Neill. He's picking me up at seven."

She wanted to ignore the surprised expression on Terence's face, but she found herself explaining.

"He *is* Aunt Margaret's Solicitor, and we do have a lot of detail which must be discussed," she said defensively.

"All right, Miss Sheila," Terence replied. "I'll tell Mr. Glendon when he calls again."

"Who's Mr. Glendon?" Sheila asked. It was a name she didn't know at all.

"He lives on Ruddance road. Moved here after you left, Miss Sheila. He's tried to interest the mistress in some business ideas."

Sheila sensed the guarded note in Terence's voice and she looked at him quickly, but he had set his face to reveal nothing.

"There's no need to see him, really," Terence added flatly. Again Sheila detected a strange note in Terence's voice.

"Tell him to call me after the funeral," she said. "I'm going to lie down for a while now."

She suddenly felt very tired. The recent days were catching up with her, and she stretched out on the big wide bed luxuriously. She removed her skirt and jacket and stretched out atop the covers in her bra and panties. From the bed she could look out across the moors, through the pattern of branches from the tall oak outside the window. Events had moved so quickly the past three days. And now, as she lay in the bed in which she'd slept most of her young life, watching the leaves play idly against the latticed, high-domed window, there was no longer any denying it, she was happy to be back in Doylan Hall. She had wanted to come, apparently more than she had let herself realize. But she hadn't want to return this way, with Aunt Margaret gone and the shadow of evil overlaying her happiness.

What was to become of Doylan Hall now? Sheila mused. What if it were willed to her? Aunt Margaret had often hinted at that. Would she stay on here? And what of her career in New York? It was almost funny how remote all that seemed now, how unimportant. In but a few short hours she had found a special kind of happiness here in Duncavan, the happiness that springs from the constancy of people and places that stand fast. Her thoughts suddenly catapulted back to those golden days when she and Brian were engaged. It had all seemed so clear to her, and, she had thought, to him. But they had each been carrying such different ideas without really ever discussing them with one another. It all came back so clearly, so terribly clearly. She had gone to Dublin and then to London to study fashion design while Brian, the young solicitor, had started on his own in Duncavan. Oh, they had casually discussed how America was the real heart of mass fashion design, and how so many more opportunities existed there for beginners. But when she had told Brian her plans to go to America, to the heart of the fashion industry, he was taken completely by surprise. She recalled how hurt and disappointed and angered she had been at his attitude. She had just assumed he would be as excited as she was to begin his law career in the land of opportunity. But he had had totally opposite thoughts, and that afternoon's confrontation danced before her eyes once again.

"America?" he had repeated incredulously. "I'm not going to America, Sheila. I want to practice here in Duncavan. There are entirely too many who flee this land for America when it's here they should be bringing what they've learned. There are people here who need help, there are things here that need straightening, there are opportunities here that wait for the taking."

"Not for me, there aren't," she remembered saying. "I can't do what I want to do here."

"And why not?" he had asked. "Use the traditions, the colors, the costumes of Connemara in your designs. Dublin and London, even Paris, they're all only a few hours by plane, if you need to go there."

But she wouldn't hear of it, Sheila recalled. It was America she would conquer. They quarreled bitterly, each accusing the other of not loving enough and not caring enough, and so it had all ended in anger and bitterness and tears and all the words too newly uttered to take back. Their engagement was broken, and she left for New York as soon as she could, where she at once drew upon those very things Brian had talked about, the designs, the colors and traditions of the people she had grown up with and knew so very well.

Sheila let her thoughts wander back to those first days when she had arrived in New York, determined, eager and more than a little angry at the world. She had found a small apartment on the lower East Side of the city, not much more than a room and a bath, with just enough space to set up a drawing board. But she had brought something new to the fashion world, and they had recognized its worth. Within six months she was living in the fashionable east seventies of New York, with her own spacious apartment and an ever-widening, ever-increasing circle of friends. She had found success and all that goes with success: acclamation, comforts, new friends. Her life was fast-moving, crowded with work, glamour, parties and romances all mixed together in one breathless existence. And she had plunged into it with a determination not only to prove herself but to wipe out the past. But as she had come to know these last days, a past that is not really past is impossible to erase. How much, she mused, had the unburied past really affected her two major romances, unbeknownst to her at the time? What under-the-surface, psychological pressures dictated not only her decision, but her choices in regard to Harrison and to Neil? There had been many romances, many men, but she had become engaged to only two. The first had been Neil, tall, glamorous, terribly handsome, a fast-rising young advertising account executive. Neil and she had become almost a newspaper columnist's staple item as they went from one social event to another. And then one night, very late, on their way home from a formal affair, Neil had given her a sideways glance as they stopped before her apartment building.

"You're not really at all interested in getting married, my girl," he had said. Sheila recalled how her eyebrows had gone up in surprise.

"What makes you say a thing like that, Neil?" she protested.

"Because it's true," he said quietly. "From the time we got engaged, you've never said another word about marriage. You're so busy working, designing, achieving success after success, and I'm so busy with ad clients, that we hardly ever talk during the days. At nights we're on a whirl of one mad party after another. And that's the way you want it. You don't want time for anything more."

"Aren't you having fun?" she countered.

"Sure, plenty of fun," he had said. "So much fun that I don't know if either of us wants to change it."

"Maybe you're right," she had said as she got out of the car. "Maybe you're right."

And so her engagement to Neil had ended, on a friendly, mutually agreeable note. They had dated numerous times afterward, in fact. Harrison came along about six months later. He was the very young, very good-looking president of half a dozen corporations, originally set up in business by his family but doing fabulously on his own. They were very different in some ways, Harrison and Neil, but very alike in one. Where Neil was dry martinis, Harrison was straight Scotch. Where Neil was brittle and charming, Harrison was serious and affable. Neil was dry and witty and stylish, Harrison was sincere and serious and thoughtful. Yet they were alike in one important thing: both were entirely caught up in their own fast-moving worlds. Her engagement to Harrison was in actuality a protracted series of weekend dates, more often than not spent at one or another formal dinner or country-club dance. During the week he was flying around the country in his own plane, visiting various plants and factories.

It had been an offhand remark by Harrison, actually intended as a compliment, a mark of appreciation, which had opened her eyes to the wrongness of it all. He had just returned from a trip, and they were dancing at a country club.

"You're a wonderful girl, Sheila," he had said. "So different from others. You don't complain at all about my having to be away every week, and when I get back you don't go on about how soon we'll get married. You really understand, darling."

The full import of what he had said struck her as a cyclone strikes a shack, shattering it completely; only it wasn't a cyclone but a clean wind, a cleansing, eye-opening blow. She recalled how Harrison, poor chap, had been utterly shocked by her reply.

"It's not a matter of understanding, Harrison," she had said seriously, soberly. "It's that I just don't give a damn."

"What are you saying, Sheila?" he had questioned, frowning, incredulous.

"I'm saying, darling, that I don't really care enough to care, and we're not engaged any more. The truth is that you don't care either, not in the right way. You want a wife because it's

something someone in your position should have, and you probably want heirs to your business. But you're really married to
your corporations."

She had walked off, leaving him standing there with his
mouth open. There was no bitterness, not on her part, at least,
and secretly, she felt certain, Harrison knew she had been right.
And now, here in Duncavan, she could see why she had chosen
to become engaged to two such men. Like her own, their lives
were filled with success but empty of happiness. But she must
have always remembered, somewhere deep in her subconscious,
something her aunt had told her long before she ever went to
America.

"Sheila," Aunt Margaret had said, "if ever there's an emptiness inside you, don't make the mistake of thinking you can fill it
with another empty soul. So many make that mistake, my child,
but an empty well cannot fill another empty well. Find someone
with a full heart and an overbrimming spirit. Only then can your
emptiness be filled."

Could she find that back here in Duncavan? Sheila asked
herself. Can you put roots back into a soil from which you've
torn them? Or was there nothing left here in this quiet land but a
dread evil? She had come back … but to what?

She fell asleep with the warm sun streaming across her figure, a golden blanket over her slender shape.

CHAPTER THREE

She awakened suddenly, sitting straight up on the bed and peering at the tall cedar and pine grandfather clock in the corner of the room. "Six o'clock!" she gasped. Brian was due at seven, and unless he'd changed he'd be prompt.

She flew into the bathroom, shedding bra and panties on the way, and turned on the bath faucets. The water flowed in with agonizing slowness. That hadn't changed, either, she thought in exasperation. While she waited, she brushed her hair and piled it up atop her head in a series of swirls. If she were careful, she might avoid getting it wet and having to do it all over again. Finally the tub was full, and she sank into the warm water, wishing she had more time to relax in it. She allowed herself five minutes more than she should have and eyed the clock as she flew into her underthings. Should she wear something very New York and smart? No, she decided. She chose a tailored suit, one of her own designs, of a deep blue and green-flecked nubby cloth. She slipped it on with a sigh of satisfaction just as she heard the heavy knocker on the door and then Brian's voice. She checked her purse to make certain the letters were there and hurried out. Brian was in the entrance hall, exchanging small talk with Terence, and she secretly smiled as she saw the approval in his eyes. It was Terence who spoke first.

"I told Mr. Glendon you'd be out for the evening. I gave Bridgit the night off, too. Have a nice evening, Miss Sheila."

"It's a business evening," Sheila commented, flashing Brian a glance. "Isn't it, Brian?"

"It is," was all he said as she walked with him to where he had a dark-green MG waiting with the top down.

"Shall I put it up for you?" he asked as Sheila slid into the seat.

"Oh, no, please don't," she answered. "I like it this way."

"Well, it's got a good heater we can put on if you get a chill."

"Where are we going?" Sheila asked. "Does the Glenderry Bairn still exist?"

"Aye," Brian said as the engine throbbed into life. "And it's still the best place, if you want to drive that far."

"Only a half-hour across the valley, if I remember," Sheila commented.

He gave a soft laugh, and the little car roared down the driveway, taking the sharp turn to the valley road on two wheels. Sheila settled back, letting her head rest against the top of the seat. It was dark already, and the ever-present mists of the valley were beginning to rise from the ground. Riding with Brian had always been a strangely satisfying thing. She always felt so very close to him, without the need to utter a word. Only the gray-dawn meetings at the beach held that same silent communication.

"How many times have we ridden through this valley, Brian?" she asked idly. "I've often thought about it. What was it Sara Teasdale said about memory? 'Better than the minting of a gold-crowned king, is the safe memory of a lovely thing.' Do you ever think back on those times, Brian?"

"Never," he said.

"Liar."

She was glad to see the quick smile that crossed his face. All too soon, the car pulled up before a long, low-roofed inn, heavy oak beams framing the white stone walls. Sheila was glad she had worn the heavy tweed; the night air had turned very brisk. Inside, they found a small table by the window, not far from the warmth of the wide-mouthed fireplace that ran alongside the front wall. They ordered drinks, rye for Brian, Scotch for her.

"Is that one of your designs you're wearing?" Brian asked with a quiet smile.

"Why, yes, as a matter of fact. I hadn't thought you'd noticed," Sheila said blandly.

"Now it's my turn to say liar," Brian countered dryly. "It's very good-looking. I can see why you've been a success in the glamorous world of fashion in New York. Oh, I know all about the doings of one Sheila McCloud, New York fashion designer. Your aunt made sure to give me regular and frequent reports."

"And what did she tell you?"

"All sorts of newsy little items, mostly the good, you can be sure. News of new successes, new contracts, special recognition. You were always doing fabulously, and of course were very happy. She did mention two broken engagements, so I imagine there must have been a few clouds some place. Or were those just going on with a bad habit?"

She felt the stinging sarcasm of the last remark. Instantly, her Irish temper flared, and she struck back.

"Did it bother you a great deal?" she asked innocently. "I mean, my being a success?"

"Yes, at first, anyway. I wanted you to fail, to come running back."

His honesty shriveled her anger.

"I'm sorry I said that. I didn't mean to dredge up old hurts."

"It was my fault. I started it," he replied. "It's unimportant now. We've more immediate things to talk about. After the funeral tomorrow, I'll come to the Hall and go through the things in your aunt's room. I'm thinking I'll find the will there. If you don't mind, that is."

"Mind?" Sheila said. "I'll be grateful to you for being there. I know I'll be in bad shape by then. I've tried not to think about tomorrow, as if it weren't really going to happen."

"You said there was something you wanted to talk to me about, something bothering you. There was, if I recall, a ring of mystery and ominousness in your voice."

There was laughter in his eyes. Did he think she'd made it up as an excuse to see him for dinner? She would demolish that quickly and forcefully.

"Aunt Margaret's death was no accident!"

There, she'd finally said it out loud. She'd finally given voice to the certainty that had grown inside her. Brian frowned and searched her eyes with a look of tolerant amusement as one might regard a slightly retarded child. She felt her temper rising. When she met his glance coolly, unwaveringly, his frown deepened.

"You're serious, aren't you?" he said. "You really mean that."

"I really mean that," she echoed.

Brian drained his glass and set it down with a shake of his head.

"Do you know what you're saying, Sheila?" he asked. "It's an ugly thing you're saying, and it's called by an ugly word ... *murder.*"

"That is precisely what I am saying."

"Frankly, Sheila, I'd like to know how, after you've been back in Duncavan for one night and a day, you can come out with such an accusation. I presume you have some kind of justification for it. I'd certainly like to hear it, whatever it is."

She had expected some initial skepticism, but he made it sound as though she'd taken leave of her senses. She felt her cheeks grow hot as she took the letters from her purse and waved them under Brian's startled nose.

"These will do for a start! They are Aunt Margaret's last two letters to me."

She unfolded the first and spread it on the table in front of him. She had read it so many times that the lines leaped out at her as he read.

Dear Sheila:

I fear this will not be my usual letter, full of news and gossip about people and places. Forgive me if I ramble, but I have not slept well for many nights. Dear child, your last letter said you might visit me soon. Make that visit right away, tomorrow, if you can. I need you here.

For the first time in my life, I am afraid. Each day I become more convinced that there is something monstrous here in Duncavan, and I fear for my life. Yet I cannot speak out until I have more proof.

If I did so now, with only my suspicions, certain of them as I am, I should be laughed at. My words would be called the senile imaginings of an old woman. So I need more time, but I may not have it. If you were here, I could make you see what I have come to believe. I have only hinted at it to Terence, for I don't want to alarm him unnecessarily as yet.

Please write and tell me you're coming. I cannot urge you enough.

Love ... Aunt Margaret.

"I wrote and told her I'd come," Sheila went on. "But I couldn't get free as quickly as I'd hoped. There were contracts to finish, loose ends to tie up and a whole host of minor problems.

Time goes so very quickly, and two weeks had slipped by when I received this."

Sheila placed the second letter carefully atop the first one.

Dear Sheila:

I had hoped you would be here by now. My worst suspicions have been proven to my satisfaction, at least. In a few days I should receive the final piece of evidence I will need to enable me to go to the authorities.

But each hour I fear more and more for my life. I'm afraid I have blundered in this unfamiliar role. Please hurry and come.

Love … Aunt M.

"That letter arrived three days ago, and I decided to move quickly. But I couldn't get a flight until yesterday, and then Terence's cable arrived in the morning. I've been sick ever since. I'll never forgive myself, never. If I'd moved faster after the first letter, this would never have happened."

Sheila broke off, aware of the tears flooding her eyes.

"Easy now, Sheila," Brian said comfortingly. "You'll not be helping anything by that. Tell me, do you have anything besides these letters?"

"Good God, aren't they enough?" she flared.

"Not for me," he answered levelly. "Do you have anything else?"

"Yes," she shot back hotly. "The simple fact that Aunt Margaret would never have fallen off the cliffs. She knew every foot of those moors as she knew her own bedroom."

"That's not a valid supposition, Sheila," Brian countered. "At night when the fog blankets the moors, anyone could miscalculate."

"Not if he knew the moors and the cliffs as Aunt Margaret knew them."

"But an old woman, alone, losing her bearings ... it's not hard to imagine how she could have strayed too near the edge."

"It's hard for me to imagine it. In fact, it's impossible for me. Look, Brian, I haven't walked the moors for seven years, and I did it today with my eyes closed. I walked from the house to the cliffs and halfway around the edge, *with my eyes closed, understand?* When you near the edge of the cliffs, you feel the wind, first. It's always there ... sun, rain, fog, day or night. It's an updraft that sweeps up the cliffs from the sea. You can tell how close you are to the edge by the strength of the wind on your face. When you're close, it blows hard, and you can hear the breakers below. Not only that, but you can tell where you're standing by the direction of the wind. Midway along the cliffs, it suddenly shifts in a funny kind of back-draft and hits you from behind. Seven years, Brian, and I still could do it with my eyes closed. Don't you see what that means?"

"It means you might have killed yourself."

"But I didn't," she added triumphantly, "and neither did Aunt Margaret."

Brian shook his head and sighed.

"Sheila, you've built a case for yourself, but I can't buy your reasoning. You're upset over what's happened over your own guilt feelings and over the letters. You're overdramatizing and searching for things."

"You still won't believe me," Sheila said, her eyes blazing. He was being the stubborn, skeptical lawyer now. "All right, she said, "let's just take the letters, then. How much more is needed?"

"A lot, I'm afraid," he answered seriously. "Yes, they are upsetting, but it seems to me you're forgetting something. Your aunt was nearing seventy-five. She has been living virtually alone since you left. An old woman can begin to imagine things. The mind can run away with itself. It's interesting that she even makes mention of that in one letter. In short, she could really have been afraid, but those fears could have been nothing but groundless fears and imagined suspicions."

"Baloney!" Sheila retorted angrily. "Aunt Margaret's mind was as sharp as a needle. I got those wonderful letters every few weeks, full of wisdom, clarity and alert, aware commentary. Doddering old woman, my ass! Yes, you heard me."

"You've not lost that blazing temper, have you?" Brian commented with a wry smile.

"No, and I haven't lost my senses, either. It was no accident. I'm convinced of that, and I'm going to prove it. If you don't want to help me, then don't!"

"Now simmer down," Brian said placatingly. "I only want to prevent you from chasing something that doesn't exist. If you're right, of course I'll help you. But I think this takes more mulling over than I've had a chance to give it. Murder is no word to cast about lightly, lass. Let me sleep on it, and tomorrow, after the funeral, we'll go over it again. I'm not convinced of anything, but I'll approach it with an open mind if you promise you'll do the same. Fair enough?"

"Fair enough," she relented. "And while we eat, you can fill me in on something else that threw me today. I went into town this morning, and I guess I saw just about everyone in Duncavan proper. It was fun, and most people were at least polite, and a lot were very glad to see me."

"Why not?" Brian commented, and there was laughter in his eyes. He knew very well what she meant.

"Anyway," she went on, "I had a really unnerving run-in with that man Bayliss; you know, the one Aunt Margaret has tending the game preserve across the valley."

"*Had* tending the game preserve," Brian said.

"Had?" Sheila questioned. "That's interesting. But first let me tell you what happened."

Quickly, Sheila recounted what had taken place, and Brian listened quietly and attentively.

"There was hatred in his eyes when he told me to get out of Duncavan," Sheila concluded. "Pure hatred."

"Bayliss has been feuding bitterly with your aunt ever since she fired him. He wanted to buy the land for a group of hunting and tourist lodges. He had the backing of some sizable money, but your aunt refused to sell. When she found out he had been letting hunters use the preserve for a healthy fee, she fired him and hailed him into court. She eventually decided not to press charges, but she swore she'd blacklist him in every part of Connemara, and he swore he'd get even with her. It was thoroughly nasty. I know, because I handled the case."

"Knowing this, you still can think Aunt Margaret's death an accident? The whole thing's completely clear to me now."

"My God, girl," Brian said, "you don't jump to conclusions; you leap at them like a trapeze artist."

"And you're still so damnably stubborn," Sheila pouted. Brian was grinning now. He was still damnably handsome, too.

"We'll not be talking about it any more tonight, remember?" he said.

"All right, not about that," Sheila replied. "But there are two more things I do want to know more about. Who is this Mr. Glendon who called this afternoon? Terence said he was someone who had tried to interest Aunt Margaret in some business propositions."

"Very possible that he did," Brian said. "She didn't mention them to me, but that wasn't at all unusual. Harry Glendon lives a few miles south of Duncavan, and I expect I know why he called you. The poor man's been a child of tragedy ever since he moved here a few months after you left. He and his wife had been here only a week when their skiff overturned offshore and she drowned. She couldn't swim, and he can't, either. He managed to cling to the boat and was finally washed ashore. A year or so ago he remarried, and only a few months back the poor woman fell from the cliffs in the fog one night as she was returning from Duncavan. I wager he called to extend his sympathies to you. No doubt he feels a close sympathy in view of what recently happened to his own wife. It probably brought his tragedy back to him again so terribly vividly."

"I see," Sheila replied. She was going to add that Mrs. Glendon's tragic accident didn't change her opinion one bit in regard to what had happened to Aunt Margaret. But the waitress brought dinner, and she decided to say nothing further about that. They ate leisurely, and Brian filled her in on all the local events of any importance, and she managed to relax and enjoy herself. She was saving her last question not so much out of cleverness, or an attempt to pick the right moment, but because she didn't know quite how to approach it. Finally, over a brandy, she told him about meeting Marla Culchane in Duncavan that afternoon. When she told him of the venom in Marla's eyes, he smiled faintly and leaned back, his own thoughts plainly absorbing his attention.

"Have you been seeing Marla?" Sheila finally said, blurting it out, annoyed at her own clumsiness.

"Marla is somewhat of a problem," he began slowly. Sheila felt her heart sinking.

"Then you have been seeing her," she said. "No wonder she flew at me like that. Are you engaged, or do you have some private understanding?"

"Whoa! Back up." Brian smiled. "I didn't say anything of the kind. I said only that Marla is somewhat of a problem. It's boon seven long years, you well know, Sheila, and Marla still lives alone with her mother, just as she did then. She has met me at a number of dances, village festivals, private parties, but that's all. I've never dated her. I've never taken her out on a date, though I've seen her home from a few places we've both been."

Brian sat back in his chair and looked uncomfortable, almost embarrassed.

"I don't really know how to say this without sounding like a conceited ass," he said. "But Marla is still in love with me, or at least she says she is. She's told me so frankly and openly. She says she has plenty of time and patience, and she'll wait until I turn to her."

"She is an attractive girl," Sheila remarked. And then, unable to resist it, she added another question: "Just why haven't you turned to her, Brian?"

She saw a slow, quiet smile form on his lips and his eyes narrow as he glanced at her.

"That, my dear Sheila McCloud, is one of those innocent little questions that are anything but innocent."

"All right. To use a legal phrase, we'll strike that question." Sheila laughed. "But I can see now why Marla hates me. My return here has not only raked up the past for her but also threatens the future. She's in love with you, and her insecurity is showing."

"That's an oversimplification, Sheila," Brian said seriously. "I don't think Marla is in love with me, not really. I think she is consumed by vengeance and bitterness over what happened seven years ago. Marrying me would be a revenge for her, upon both of us, I guess. I've watched that girl over the years, and I've been saddened and concerned by her increasing bitterness, her sullen moodiness. I've heard it from others. Young fellows have dated her, some new to Duncavan, and word gets around, you know. She seems constantly to be preoccupied with thoughts of her own, and she's subject to sudden, unreasonable fits of anger and nastiness. Every time I've been with her, she's been most pleasant and gay, but I feel those times have been masks, nothing but masks."

"I feel sorry for her then, Brian," Sheila said honestly.

"So do I," Brian agreed. "But we all have crosses to bear. It's how we bear them that counts."

His eyes were suddenly tender and warm, and when they finally headed back across the valley, now thick with mist, she snuggled closer to him in the little MG. She found herself hoping that you could go home again, that you could pick up sticks. At Doylan Hall, only the entrance light was on, and Brian made no move to come in.

"Good night, Sheila McCloud," he said softly, and Sheila hoped that what she saw in his eyes was really there. She let herself in quietly, and went straight to her room and into bed. She thought of all the things they had talked about and of the man Dayliss, as her flesh grew cold with sudden fright. He had sworn vengeance on her aunt, and there had been hatred in his eyes, enough for murder. She was sure of that. If Aunt Margaret had been waiting for some further evidence, she had found it and forced the man to act. Sheila knew she had to retrace her aunt's steps, somehow to discover those same things which had made her aunt fear for her life.

Marla Culchane crept into her thoughts, also. The girl hated her, but it was an intensely personal thing, she imagined. It was hard to see where Marla's feelings could or would involve Aunt Margaret. So she pushed thoughts of the girl off into a corner of her mind. Sheila lay back on the soft bed and made herself think of other things. The leaves rustled against the roof and stroked the windows. It had been a long time since she had slept with the sound of leaves in the night wind. Too long, she sighed. Finally she fell asleep.

CHAPTER FOUR

Sheila awoke and slowly, reluctantly, began to dress, glad for the silence of the great house, a silence particularly fitting on this day. And this day was now at hand. There was no time left to turn away. She hadn't gone to the funeral parlor. The casket was closed, anyway. But the truth was that she had to find the courage for this day. She put on the simple black high-necked dress she had managed to pick up only an hour before plane time, thanks to one of the dress houses she knew well. It was a size too small, but the only non-mini-dress she could find. Black shoes and a small black hat with a short veil encircling a narrow brim completed her outfit. Finished, she stood quietly, an overwhelming sadness upon her, enveloped in that feeling of utter helplessness that comes at those times when a person stands before eternal truths. Her insides had turned into a dull nothingness as she made her way downstairs into the main hall and into the great drawing room to stand before the painting. The service would of course be at St. Francis Xavier, with Father Thomaseen officiating. Now the girl knelt down and, with bowed head, said her own private goodbyes, with only the great room to hear her quiet sobs and only the painting to look down upon her tears.

Finally she got to her feet and walked from the room without looking back. It was time to find Terence and start for Duncavan. She would have preferred to walk to St. Francis, but it might be a little too much for the old man. They'd use one of the cars. The door to Terence's room was closed. She paused and knocked.

There was no answer. Perhaps he was outside with the car. She went to the narrow hallway window and peered out. The driveway was empty, and she could see the garage doors were closed. She pushed open the kitchen door and found no one there. She went back and knocked on the door of his room again. Carefully she tried the doorknob and called his name. The door swung open to reveal an empty, barren room, the lamp still lighted. The cedar chests that had lined the walls were gone; the closets stood open and barren. Then she saw the note propped up on the small round table beneath the lamp. Her hand trembled as she picked it up.

Dear Miss Sheila:

I am sorry to do this, but I could not stay for the funeral. It is too much for an old man to bear. I cannot stay at Doylan Hall without Lady Margaret.

I am going far away where I will meet no one to remind me of Lady Margaret and Doylan Hall. It is the only way for me. Forgive me, but I know you will understand.

Respectfully, Terence.

Sheila bit her lower lip and felt the harshness of her breathing. She fought back the tears. The old wooden dresser stood with each drawer hanging emptily, forlornly. Coat hangers strewn on the closet floor added their own touch of finality. Slowly she left the room. It was something she never would have expected of Terence. She somehow felt letdown. She had been certain that he would have stayed, no matter how painful it might have been. There had always been that steadfastness, that devotion in his character. But perhaps seven years changes a man's character. She thrust the note in her purse and then suddenly paused at the doorway. Turning, she ran back into the room. This time when she emerged her eyes burned with a strange brightness and she half-ran from the house. She opened the garage doors. It was too late to walk now. The old Rolls was in front, the keys, as always, in the glove compartment. She drove quickly, almost recklessly, through the empty streets of the village.

The church was overflowing when she arrived, passing quickly under the black-draped arch of the door. She saw Brian turning in the front pew, looking for her as she made her way down the aisle, head held high. The entire town seemed to have come, and she searched the sea of faces as she walked. She noted her fourth cousin, Grace Lyons, beside her great-uncle, Regis Cluny. It had been many years since she had seen either of them. The man Bayliss was nowhere in sight. She had half-expected him to be clever enough to appear. As she sat down beside Brian, Father Thomaseen took his place before the altar, and she heard the priest begin the solemn words of the funeral mass.

"Where's Terence?" Brian whispered. Without looking up, Sheila pushed the note into his hands.

"Eternal rest give to them, O Lord; and let perpetual light shine upon them," she heard the priest intone to muffled sobs from the congregation. But there were no tears for Sheila now, only whirling thoughts and a knotted, quivering stomach. She heard hardly any of the service as her mind raced wildly, and she was conscious of Brian's frequent glances at her set face and tightened lips. Soon enough she found herself standing on the steps outside, receiving the condolences of each one who passed until their faces became a formless blur and she wished they would all go away. Her cousin and uncle told her where they were staying in town, and she promptly forgot where. Then an unfamiliar face halted before her, a fairly stout man of medium height. She was immediately held by the terrible sadness of his deep-set brown eyes, eyes that mirrored a deep anguish. His voice was slow and soft.

"I'm Harry Glendon, my dear," he said. "I know how you feel more than any of the others. My deepest sympathios. I hope we can have a chat together sometime soon."

"Thank you," Sheila murmured. "Please call me in a few days."

Harry Glendon pressed her hand consolingly, and his eyes seemed to deepen even more as he turned away.

With Brian beside her, she reached the cemetery and stood with the small cluster of figures. She saw without seeing, walked without walking and heard without hearing until all the grim business was finally done with and she found herself back at Doylan Hall. Father Thomaseen had returned with them and stayed for tea. When he left, Sheila sank back onto the deep sofa of the drawing room and closed her eyes. Brian took Terence's note from his pocket.

"I'm terribly sorry about this," he said. "I know it must have made things harder for you. I noticed how grim you were during the service, almost as though you were trying to make anger push out grief."

"That's exactly what I was doing," Sheila replied.

"Poor Terence. He must be in his own private hell. His devotion to your aunt was a lifelong thing. I'll try to get a lead on where he might have gone to, relatives or some such thing."

Sheila sat up straight.

"Terence had no relatives," she said, "and he didn't *go* anywhere. He was taken from here last night. He's probably dead by now."

"Sheila! What in God's name has gotten into you?" Brian exploded. "You've got a murder complex. You've some sort of obsession. I'm really getting worried about you!"

"Obsession, is it?" Sheila shouted back, leaping to her feet. "Come with me."

She grabbed Brian's arm and pulled him into Terence's room, gesturing to the empty closets, the barren walls, the gaping dresser drawers.

"Emptied! Gone ... everything gone," she said, feeling her breasts strain under the tightness of the black dress. "He cleared out, his pipe collection, his clothes, everything!"

"What's unusual about that? Of course he'd take his precious personal belongings."

Striding to Terence's little desk, Sheila tore open the top drawer, reached back into the deepest corner and pulled out the meerschaum pipe.

"This is what's wrong," she fairly shouted. "This, his favorite among all favorite pipes, the meerschaum that once belonged to Thomas Moore ... it's still here. He never kept it with the others because he smoked it so often. A man clears out, taking all his belongings except the one thing most treasured by him? Never!"

Sheila turned the pipe in her fingers and took a firmer grip on herself. She had come close to cracking just then, and that was the last thing she wanted to do.

"Terence would never leave this," she continued. "Don't you see, it was made to look as though Terence had cleared out. I even believed it for a while. But I just couldn't accept it ... not of Terence. The killer overlooked this because it wasn't with the others. Or maybe he found it and, because it was stuck away in the drawer, thought it was something Terence would leave behind."

"But the note," Brian said carefully. "Didn't you recognize Terence's handwriting?"

"I've never seen Terence's handwriting. I doubt that Aunt Margaret had or anyone else. With no relatives and no distant friends, he had no cause to write anyone. Oh, Brian, it's crystal clear. Bridgit was off last night, and we were at dinner. The killer had a perfect chance to strike."

"Well, I must admit this disturbs me," Brian said, his face reflecting a frown of concern. "I still believe your aunt's letters could be the result of imagined fears, but now ... well, frankly, I really don't know what to think."

"You don't know what to think?" Sheila cried out in exasperation. "Aren't you carrying skepticism a bit far? How plain do you want things, Brian O'Donnell? It's as plain as the Rock of Cashel, that's what it is. With all your doubts, it's Thomas you should be, not Brian. But I know what I know, and I'll not be thinking otherwise."

She had slipped back into the speech rhythms of her girlhood as easily as one slips into a comfortable old coat. She glared at the man before her, whose face suddenly erupted in a broad smile.

"Don't explode," he said. "You did promise you'd listen to me, you know."

"I'm listening." Sheila glowered over folded arms.

"I still say that murder requires an awfully powerful motive," Brian began. "People just don't go about committing murder in cold blood unless they have a deep motive or they're psychopaths. I can't think of anyone in Duncaven who fits either of those roles."

"The man, Bayliss," Sheila snapped. "Didn't you tell me yourself that he swore vengeance? And if I ever saw hatred in his eyes, I saw it yesterday. I'd say he is a psychopath."

"No," Brian countered. "An angry man, a hating man, a vengeful and bitter man, but a psychopath ... no! I'm certain he could and would be capable of causing a lot of trouble. I'm certain he could even be a violent man. I'm equally certain that he'd try to get back at your aunt in some way. I'm certain he could do a lot of terrible and vengeful things. But cold-blooded murder? No, I just don't see it in the man."

"Anyone is capable of murder," Sheila said. "Criminal experts and psychiatrists have found that out long ago. And I'll give you the motive. Aunt Margaret had found out something about him, something terrible and frightening. That was what she was waiting final proof of. I'm going to find out what it was if I have to turn all of Connemara upside down."

"Then why was Terence done away with as you claim? Where's the motive there?"

"The killer was afraid Aunt Margaret might have confided her fears to Terence. He wasn't taking any chances."

Brian walked to the tall latticed windows and gazed out at the bright sunshine.

"It's hard for me to believe it, but if you are right," he said, "you may be in danger, too. At this moment I don't know what to think, but we'll have to proceed on the assumption that you may be right."

He turned to Sheila and took her shoulders in his hands. His touch was warm and reassuring, and she wanted very much to bury herself in his chest as she used to do. But she held herself very still as Brian looked seriously into her eyes.

"I want you to stay in close touch with me," he commanded. "I don't want you to go anywhere or do anything without telling me about it first. If you come onto anything you think important, I want you to let me know right away. I don't know if you should stay here at Doylan Hall."

"Bridgit will be here with me," Sheila replied. "Besides, I must stay here if I'm to find out what it was Aunt Margaret knew. This is the logical place to be."

"I suppose so," Brian said, dropping his hands from her shoulders. "But I'd better start searching for that will. I'd asked

Terence to lock Lady Margaret's room and touch nothing. Do you know where the keys are kept!"

"A master set was always kept in the butler's pantry. I'll go look."

Sheila returned in a few minutes with a set of keys on a large, round wire ring.

"Success," she announced. "Let's see if the room is still locked. After last night, who knows?"

"This would be a good time for you to begin going through Lady Margaret's personal belongings, Sheila. You'd be the one she'd want to do it. It's a grim business. So if you'd rather not, I'll have everything carted out, sorted and anything important delivered back to you."

"No, I'll do it," Sheila answered. "I didn't want to tackle it so soon, but now, in a way, everything that's happened has made it easier for me. It's given me a purpose, something to search for in memory of Aunt Margaret."

Her aunt's room was at the top of the stairs, still locked, and Sheila steeled herself against the sudden rush of tears as they entered. The bed was made, the heavy deep green drapes pulled back to let the sun stream into the large, airy room. Along one wall was a tall, sturdy bookcase, and facing it on the opposite wall, the big, heavy oaken dresser. Sheila saw the picture of herself atop the dresser. Almost against the middle window was her aunt's desk, inlaid with rosewood on teak.

"I'll start with the desk," Brian said. "She kept most of her papers and business documents filed away in the drawers."

As Sheila opened the top drawer of the dresser, she saw Brian systematically begin to empty each drawer of the desk. Soon he had a stack of land deeds, leases, letters and assorted business papers piled high on an adjoining chair.

"I'll have to go through all these in my office," he murmured. The big dresser had revealed nothing except personal effects. Sheila made neat stacks of the various things on the dresser top and finally closed the bottom drawer with a sigh. Just then Brian cried out.

"I've found it," he said, holding aloft a thick fold of paper. "Right here at the bottom of everything. I'll take this, file it officially and set a date for the formal reading."

"When will that be, Brian?"

"It ought to be soon. There are very few who need to be notified to attend. Really, only your cousin Grace Lyons and your great-uncle Cluny. They're both here, as you know. And yourself, of course. I'll try to set it in a few days, Thursday, perhaps. I've got to go to Dublin on business tomorrow, overnight, but I'll be back Wednesday and see to it at once."

At the door, Brian turned and looked deeply into Sheila's eyes.

"Remember, you're to stay in close touch with me, and don't do anything foolish. See that the house is well bolted at night. And keep your supsicions to yourself. If you're right about all this, and the killer knows you are suspicious, you'll be in more danger."

"But you're still not convinced?"

"Let's say I'm convinced enough not to take any chances. If it turns out I'm right, nothing is lost by our being careful."

He paused and ran one hand over Sheila's face, ever so lightly.

"Take care, mind you now," he said gruffly. Once again she wanted to lean into his arms, but he had given her no indication of anything other than friendship. She felt he was holding back, waiting for her to give the first sign, but was he, really? Or was she only letting herself think that because it was what she wanted to believe? She stepped back. She wasn't going to add embarrassment to her other problems.

"I'll be careful," she said. "Call me when you get back."

"First thing, you can be sure," he said, and was off down the few steps to the driveway. Sheila let the heavy door swing closed and slowly went back to her aunt's room. She went through the closets, putting the dresses and coats in separate stacks on the bed. They were all in quite good condition. She would call Father Thomaseen. There were plenty of poor in Connemara who could use them. When she'd finished, she shut the closets and closed the room. Brian had been right. It was a grim, depressing business, and she felt tired, very tired. She went downstairs and met Bridgit in the hallway with a tray of tea and biscuits.

"I thought you might be needing this," the woman said. "Where do you want to have it, Miss Sheila?"

"In the kitchen," Sheila exclaimed. "I always used to love tea in the kitchen, and I can talk to you at the same time."

While she sipped her tea, Bridgit told her of her last four years at Doylan Hall, and Sheila found herself liking the pleasant woman. She turned out to be a solid, comfortable kind of person. The cook chatted away, trying to let talk and sheer sound fill the void of sorrow.

"You will stay on, won't you, Bridgit?" Sheila heard herself asking. "At least until the will is read and we learn more about what will happen to Doylan Hall?"

"Of course," Bridgit replied. "I'd hoped you would want it that way."

When Sheila had finished the tea, she felt better but still weary.

"I'm going to rest until dinner," she told the cook. "And I know I won't be hungry then. Just fix a cold snack I can nibble at later."

"All right, Miss Sheila," Bridgit said. "Here's the mail. The postman brought it about an hour ago. There are some things addressed to Lady Margaret. I knew you'd want to handle them yourself."

Sheila took the mail and went to her room. She pulled off the black dress and hung it in the farthest corner of the big closet. She stretched out on the big bed in her slip. Most of the mail was the usual assortment of handbills and circulars, a notice of the annual board meeting of the Dublin Symphony, one of her aunt's lifelong interests, and one large manila envelope. Sheila opened it and brought out a letter and two newspapers.

"*BRADLEY TRACING, LTD.*, the letterhead announced in bold type. "*Back issues of all newspapers our specialty.*"

Sheila read the letter obviously memeographed on the stationery.

"Dear Customer:
    We enclose the back issues of the newspapers you inquired about. Thank you for your prompt payment.
                    Respectfully,
                        Bradley Tracing, Ltd."

Sheila unfolded the two journals. One was the *London Daily Express* of May 12, 1966. The other was the *Irish Times* of June 21, 1960. Holding the newspapers, Sheila could think of but one thing: were these two newspapers the final piece of evidence Aunt Margaret had been waiting for? Sheila was certain they were as she furiously scanned the pages of news, advertisements, special interest sections and "personal" columns. But the newspapers revealed nothing. If they held a key, it was well buried.

Of course, Sheila told herself angrily. I don't know what I'm looking for. I wouldn't recognize what is vital in these pages if it screamed out at me. I've got to uncover whatever it was Aunt Margaret uncovered, first.

She carefully folded the two newspapers and put them in the drawer of the bureau, under her blouses and sweaters, certain they held secrets yet to be unlocked. She lay back on the bed again, forced her mind to stop its incessant whirling and finally fell asleep to be awakened, hours later, by Bridgit's knock.

"Are you all right, Miss Sheila?" she heard Bridgit call. The room was dark. Sheila lit the lamp, slipped on a robe and opened the door to see the honest concern on the older woman's face.

"I'm sorry," she said sleepily. "I had no idea I'd sleep so long."

"I thought you had fallen asleep, and I didn't want to waken you," Bridgit answered. "But when it got late, well, I just decided it best to come and look. That cold snack you wanted is waiting."

"Thank you, Bridgit," Sheila said. "I'll come right down."

"If you won't be needing anything else, I'll be going to my room," Bridgit stated.

"By all means," Sheila said, and she reached out to touch Bridgit's sleeve. "Thank you for staying on here with me. It's very comforting."

Bridgit gave her a glance of understanding and was off. Sheila found the snack in the kitchen and sat down to eat, because she knew she had to eat. Tomorrow, she mused, would be spent continuing the unpleasant but necessary task of going through her aunt's belongings. In the afternoon she'd drive across Mara Valley to the game preserve. If Aunt Margaret had discovered something damaging to the man, Bayliss, perhaps some clue, some lead could be found there. It might be nothing more than a pleasant drive, but she had to begin looking somewhere. That was as good a place as any. There was a gamekeeper's house where he had lived on the property. She'd go over every inch of it.

Besides, if the trip proved futile, it would at least be a happy homecoming of sorts. She recalled how she used to spend whole days there alone, walking through the thick forests, sunning herself beside the small ponds and brooks, reveling in the wild and untrammeled land, making herself a part of the unspoiled creatures who watched her every move. She'd take the Sunbeam she'd seen in the garage and drive leisurely. When she went to bed, her plans were fully formed and she thought she would sleep soundly. Such was not to be the case. Perhaps it was the long nap which had taken the edge from her weariness, perhaps she was more tense than she'd realized, but whatever the reason, she found herself reliving every moment of the last two days, rehearing every one of Brian's words. Was she really overdramatizing? Could Aunt Margaret's letters really have been only the result of an old woman's vivid imagination? It wasn't entirely impossible, she knew. Brian knew the people of the region with a knowledge she no longer possessed after seven years. Was his evaluation of the man Bayliss a right one?

But then she thought of the desperation of Aunt Margaret's last letter, of Terence's favorite pipe, and she knew she had to continue on the basis of the conviction of her own feelings. There was, she was certain, some monstrous evil here in Duncaven. She tried to sleep again, but she kept waking at every unexpected sound: the slam of a shutter, the hard scrape of the tree branches in the wind, the hoot of an owl. It was nearing dawn when she finally lapsed into exhausted slumber.

CHAPTER FIVE

Sheila won the struggle to get up early and, donning a pair of deep red hip-huggers and a coral sweater, set about going through the rest of the things in her aunt's room. Breakfast was short, just tea and toast. This disappointed Bridgit, who had been poised to produce pancakes, sausages and all the accoutrements of a leisurely meal. Once in her aunt's room, Sheila concentrated on the physical effort involved in taking things from closets, stacking and discarding, sorting and arranging. She knew she dared not pause, or she would be overwhelmed by memories. So she kept on all morning with a grim determination that finally saw the room cleared out of things. She phoned Father Thomaseen, who promptly sent Tim O'Leary with a small burro and wagon to gather up all she had marked for him.

It was past one o'clock when she finished, and she welcomed the cold beef and coffee Bridgit had prepared. There would be a lot more to do in the huge house, and she was grateful for the opportunity it would give her to plunge herself into further sheer physical work. She knew Aunt Margaret had things tucked away in every room, and it would take time to find them all. And with it all, she would be searching for the evidence she knew must be somewhere, whatever it was that would put her on the trail of what she had to uncover. The library, with its row upon row of books, was a frightening prospect, but what she sought could conceivably be tucked into one of the books. It would be like Aunt Margaret to do that. And there was a small but heavy old safe in the corner of the library. Only Aunt Margaret had had the combination. Sheila made a mental note to call Tom Grogan in town and tell him to come with his tools and open it for her. He was a locksmith, but she was sure he had files and saws that could open the old safe. But today she had other plans.

The noon sun was still high when she took the Sunbeam and set out across the valley. She relaxed as she drove, taking the long road that circled the lough with its sparkling waters. When she reached the *drim*, the ridge of the other side of the lough, the valley rose steeply, and she turned onto the *shan* road, the old road. It wandered about five miles before she came to the weathered sign: DOYLAN HALL GAME PRESERVE. Another half-mile into the preserve, the road came to an abrupt halt in a tangle of thick roots and dense underbrush. Sheila got out, and a partridge rustled the brush as it took wing in a skipping flight. Thrusting her hands into the pockets of the hip-huggers, Sheila began to walk deeper into the forest, stepping carefully, pausing to watch every sign of the wild creatures she knew were following her progress into their domain.

A quail fluttered off on the right; a rabbit bounded across the path; and then she saw a gray fox leisurely trot out onto the path, look at her and casually move off. She rounded a bend, stepping over a fallen tree, to come upon two young does who turned their wet-brown eyes upon her before bolting away with great, bounding leaps. The thickness of the woods grew a little less as she neared the clearing where the gamekeeper's cabin sat upon a *tully*, a little hillock that overlooked the clearing.

Sheila tried the door and happily found it unlocked. The sturdy cabin of thick oak logs and heavy crisscrossed ceiling beams inside smelled of mustiness and dampness. Obviously, it had not been lived in for some while. The fireplace hadn't been cleaned, and the remains of half-burned logs and boxes still lay there. Sheila left the door open to let in the fresh air.

The interior of the cabin was divided into two sections, the larger one the first section with the fireplace and old leather sofa. The smaller second section was a sleeping area with two bunk-beds lining the walls. Sheila strolled through both sections, examining every inch of the cabin. She peered into the barrel that served as a trash basket, picking up and scanning every scrap of paper. She peered inside empty cans that littered one corner of the cabin. She turned up the mattresses on the bunks to see if there might be anything beneath them. A loose floor board caught her eye, and she lifted it to peer beneath it. Only a centipede racing from the sudden invasion of light greeted her. She took the andiron and poked about in the rubbish and ashes of the fireplace. But the cabin appeared to hold no information for her, and she sauntered outside, dejected and disappointed, yet knowing she was wrong to feel that way. She had been allowing herself to hold unwarranted hopes in expecting to come out here and just turn up some vital bit of information. The answers she sought were well hidden, and they would stay that way until she brought them to light by digging hard and long. There would be no easy way.

Strolling from the cabin, she reached a flat rock about twenty yards away at the other edge of the small clearing. She lay back, stretching out on its warm surface, feeling the burning caress of the sun through her clothes. Out of the corner of one eye she watched a woodchuck watching her. She closed her eyes and remembered how often she had lain on this rock as a girl. The sun and her fitful night's sleep combined forces, and it was only a few minutes before the girl lay fast asleep on the stone. Now she slept the deep sleep of the exhausted. The soft wind through the trees added its lullaby, and the time passed quickly.

Sheila awoke when a damp chill raced through her body. She sat up straight, startled, brushing one hand over her forehead. There was no sun now, and the night had sent its chill winds ahead. Sheila got to her feet, thoroughly annoyed with herself for having fallen asleep so long. She headed back down the *tully* and through the overgrown, dense path. Night would fall quickly up here in the woods, she knew, and she hurried, only there was no real hurrying through the heavy underbrush. Without the sun filtering its way through the thick ceiling of intertwined branches, the woods were already dark, and when she reached the car the night mists were already starting to rise from the ground in gray wisps and curls. With amazing speed they mingled together to form airborne blankets of opaqueness. She backed the Sunbeam down the path until she reached the *shan* road, where there was barely room to turn around. She switched on the headlights to reveal the mist, now become a fog which settled with increasing thickness as the night closed down with gathering speed. The old road did not allow for fast travel, and the Sunbeam rattled and shook over its bumps until she thought it would come apart.

Reaching the end of the *shan* road she slowed for the turn onto the gravel of main valley road. She thought she heard the sound of another engine and paused before turning out, waiting to see the diffused glow of headlights in the mist. But there was none, and she turned onto the road, picking up speed quickly only to find that speed was impossible. The fog was now coming in thick patches, and she had to slow down to a crawl every few minutes. Again she heard the sound of another engine, also slowing down repeatedly, and she looked through the rear-view mirror. But again there were no headlight beams to be seen. The valley road was full of curves and bends. Obviously, the other car was around one of them each time she looked back for it. As the fog cleared away for a brief moment, she saw the water as she rounded a sharp curve. She was beginning to circle the largest of the *loughs* in the valley, she realized, when suddenly she felt the Sunbeam shudder and the engine gasp. She pressed down hard on the accelerator. Instead of a surge of power, there was only another shudder, and the engine went dead. The fog had rolled over her again, but she steered the car to the side of the road, trying to guess where the road bordered the shoulder, until the Sunbeam rolled to a halt.

"Now what?" she said aloud. It had probably been foolish of her to take the Sunbeam without asking it if was in good order, she realized. She opened the door and got out to try and flag the car that was somewhere behind her. As she did so, she heard the sound of the other engine fade away. There was no turn-off on the stretch of road she had just traveled, so probably the other car had been brought to a halt by the fog. There was nothing to do now but wait. In the glove compartment of the Sunbeam she found a flashlight in working order. Snapping it on, she walked around the little car. When she reached the rear, beside the gas tank, the light revealed a trail of liquid on the ground. From the smell, it was unmistakably gasoline. Kneeling down and peering up beneath the car, Sheila turned the light onto the fuel line leading from the gas tank. As she slowly moved the light down the fuel line she saw a hole, small and neat, about two thirds of the way down the pipe. With a frown, she ran her finger over the hole, then held it under the flash. There was no trace of rust on her fingertip, and the hole felt neat and round, as if it had been made by a small punch or an awl. Then, on her knees half under the car, she heard a sound on the gravel—footsteps, careful and deliberate footsteps. She switched off the flash and quickly got to her feet, moving around to the front of the car. She stood very still, hearing her own breathing, sounding terribly loud and harsh in the mist-shrouded silence. The footsteps were coming closer, very slowly, cautiously.

Now she knew why she had seen no lights through her mirror. She had been followed, her pursuer driving without lights, picking up the red glow of her taillights. Obviously, she had been watched coming out of the game preserve, perhaps all the while she had been there. She had made it even easier by falling asleep for so long, leaving whoever it was plenty of time to punch the hole in the fuel line. There was no question in her mind as to who it was. But why hadn't he just struck while she had been asleep on the rock near the cabin? No, she realized instantly. That might have been awkward to explain. It might have aroused suspicions. This way it would be so simple, just another accident. The Sunbeam, with her inside it, would be found at the bottom of the *lough*. Simple. Neat. After all, hadn't Sheila McCloud been away for seven years so she was no longer familiar with the curving road? It was made to order for him.

Now the footsteps were almost upon her, and she saw the shadowy figure looming dimly through the fog. She wanted to shine the light on the figure, but doing so would only reveal where she stood. Besides, the fog might prevent her from seeing his face, anyway. Sheila crouched by the hood of the Sunbeam as the man's shadowy bulk began to move carefully around the car. Had he seen her? she wondered. She began to circle around the front of the Sunbeam and instantly heard the scrape of her feet on the gravel. She saw the figure half-turn and then move quickly toward her. He saw her in fog-shrouded outline just as she did him. As she turned to run, she threw the flashlight with all her strength and heard the sharp crack and cry of surprised pain. She raced headlong into the woods bordering the road, grateful for the moment's head start, only to realize that in the brush she was leaving a trail of snapping twigs and rustling leaves. Trying to run, stumbling, picking herself up and stumbling again, she ran through the woods, hearing the sound of his pursuit behind her. Branches and sharp thorns tore at her face as she rushed through the brush, and she was glad she was wearing slacks and not a skirt. The woods were no refuge, she realized unhappily. The brush was too dry and the ground too full of crackling twigs. She could not be silent enough to hide, and so she plunged on, regardless of the noise she made, hoping to stay ahead of him but hearing the sound of his pursuit coming closer. She had to find some place else, and she tried to gather her thoughts as she groped through the fog. thoughts as she groped through the fog.

She searched her memory as she tried to get her bearings. The car had stopped at the curve of the first *lough*. That would be *loughbray*, the lake at the hill. Suddenly it came back to her in a rush of remembrance. The Dolmens were near the *lough* ... they could even be soon from the curve of the road. Yes, there she could hide as she had hidden so often in games as a youngster. The Dolmens were the great Druidic monuments the hill folk called Druid's Altars or Clant's Tables. Each Dolmen was made up of three or four towering, uncarved stones standing upright, across which another huge stone, a capstone, was lain. The gigantic constructions did indeed seem to be huge altars and giant's tables, and as a girl, Sheila and her friends played hide and seek and tag among the towering stones, racing in and out and around them. If one was good at it, it was almost impossible to be caught. Yes, the Dolmens were her one hope, she realized. If she reached them first, she was confident she could stay out of his reach.

Sheila turned sharply and headed for the road, hearing her pursuer pause to listen and then change directions to follow the sound of her flight. But she had gained precious seconds, and when she reached the road she crossed to the other side, ran along the embankment for some fifty yards and then plunged into the woods on the other side. She prayed her sense of direction would hold in the fog. And then, with a feeling of gratitude and relief, she saw the Dolmens, looming up in the fog before her, great, majestic echoes of an ancient time and a long forgotten people. There were three Dolmens grouped together, each with its own horizontal capstone. She ran to the left stone of the first group and took up a position to await her pursuer. It was but a few moments until she saw his figure appear and halt, listening for her whereabouts. Then he moved forward, heading for the nearest stone of the first Dolmen. Pressed against the stone, she watched the shadowy figure move from the first to the second stone until he was at the one where she hid. As he turned the corner of the stone, she ran out, knowing he would see the silhouette of her figure but also knowing he wouldn't be able to tell which of the other stones she had chosen to hide behind. Now in the second Dolmen, pressed against the center stone, she waited silently again until finally he neared her, and once more she darted out through the huge stones to slip behind another. Once more she waited in silence, listening to him shuffle from stone to stone, hearing his harsh breathing, until he neared her. Then she raced out to dart behind still another giant hiding place. Effortlessly she slipped in and out and around the Druid's great monuments, her every move a living echo of her childhood games.

But this time, Sheila knew, death was one of the players, and as the night wore on the chill dampness of the fog infiltrated her every bone until her legs quivered with muscle cramps. Yet she matched move for move with her pursuer, knowing with grim satisfaction that she had the upper hand in this deadly game. She had to hold out till dawn came to blow away the fog. Dawn would bring travelers on the road, other cars she could see and run to from where the Dolmens stood. And most of all, dawn would end his chances of arranging another convenient "accident." He would have to flee like a banshee before the light of day. The hours seemed to wear on endlessly until suddenly Sheila became aware of a grayness creeping into the fog, turning the heavy blanket into a wet mist. Dawn was upon them!

Standing very still behind one of the stones, she heard the man utter a muffled oath and start to walk from the Dolmens. The sound of his footsteps grew fainter, but she didn't move. She was not going to be tricked at this last moment. She strained her ears, listening to the sounds of someone hurrying off through the woods. And then faintly, in the distance, she heard the sound of an engine starting. Then her entire body began to tremble, her legs suddenly lost their muscles, and she sank down beside the giant stone, unable to halt the sobs which racked her frame. Finally they subsided, and she pulled herself to her feet.

The mists were lightening rapidly, and she could see the valley road now. As she made her way through the huge echoes of another era, her foot struck against a hard object which moved with a metallic clink against a rock. She looked down to see a *slane*, a sharp, long-handled tool used in cutting peat from the bogs, Sheila picked it up and took it with her. She crossed the road and followed it back to where she had left the Sunbeam. She leaned against the car and waited, knowing that someone would be passing that way soon. Mercifully, it was only a short wait before a small Austin open-sided truck loomed into view, coming to a halt at Sheila's frantic waving. It was Cyrus O'Malley who, she instantly remembered, leased his truck and himself to Treadwell's General Store for deliveries. She met his surprised look with an explanation about a faulty fuel line, recalling Brian's words of caution. Besides, she remembered, Cyrus O'Malley had never been known for being close-mouthed. Cyrus deposited her at Doylan Hall and went on into town to send a tow-truck back for the Sunbeam.

Bridgit was just coming down the stairs when Sheila went inside.

"You're up early," the cook said in surprise. Sheila decided against explaining, even to Bridgit, at that moment. Besides, she was too exhausted.

"Yes," she answered. "I've been up early ... too early. I'm going to my room and rest awhile. Please call me if I'm not down by lunch."

"Yes, mum," the woman answered, a small frown crossing her face as she watched the girl go up the stairs.

In her room, Sheila put the *slane* in a bureau drawer, stripped off her clothes and lay naked on the bed. She crawled beneath the sheets. They felt cool and smooth and soothing against her skin. She was back, alive, and she said a small prayer of thanks before she fell asleep.

CHAPTER SIX

Bridgit's insistent pounding finally awoke the exhausted girl, and Sheila answered sleepily. The sun streaming in through the open curtains of the window beckoned invitingly and wrapped itself around her body as she emerged from the big bed. Her figure, long and lithe and beautifully molded, crossed the spacious room and, with only the bathroom mirror to see its beauty, she showered and dressed. Sheila put on a yellow shirt-waist she had designed herself. She needed something bright and cheerful. Downstairs, she had tea and toast in the kitchen with Bridgit. Her stomach was still churning, and the tea felt warm and comforting. Brian was coming for dinner, and Bridgit was busy with preliminary preparations. It was plain the cook was going to turn it into an event. Sheila walked out into the gardens that surrounded the back part of the great house. The sun was warm, the sky was very *gorm*, very blue, the birds sang sweetly in the bushes, and it seemed a lovely, peaceful world. She found a *beg cool* for herself, a little corner beside a willow tree, and sat down to drink in the quiet, calm loveliness of the spot.

The night only a few short hours before didn't seem possible. It seemed like nothing but an ugly dream, yet she knew better. Even now, in the peace and brightness of the garden, Sheila could feel the fog again and see the shadowy figure slipping in and out of the Dolmens. She shuddered in the sunlight as she again realized how close to death she had come. Twice now death had struck—at Aunt Margaret and at Terence. She would have been the third victim. When would he strike again? It was a strange and unreal race she was running with death; strange because she knew not why or how it sought her, and unreal because it just didn't seem possible for it to happen here. There are places where the spectre of evil seems natural, dark and brooding places where death seems a likely visitor. But here in the quiet, secure and stable village of Duncavan it was unthinkable. And yet, Sheila knew all too well, death was here, waiting to strike again.

Since she had come back to Duncaven she had come to realize that she wanted again to become a part of this lovely land, the land of her birth and heritage. But where it had once been a happy and comforting place, it was now a land of foreboding and dread for her. Yet she was here, and she knew what this land meant to her now. She had to stand up to this lurking, stalking spectre and conquer it. More and more she was certain her assailant of last night had to be the man Bayliss. Duncavan was not a place full of strangers and suspects. He had to be the man. She was walking in her aunt's footsteps and courting the same fate as he transferred his hatred of her aunt to her, fearful she would discover what Aunt Margaret had discovered.

Sheila rested her head against the trunk of the willow tree. She had to clear her mind, to think of something else for a while, or her head would fair explode. She was so glad Brian would be there in a few hours, she had so much to tell him. *Brian!* There was more than enough to tear her mind from her dread thoughts. Sheila got up, shook herself as a dog shakes the water from his coat, and went back into the house. She'd help Bridgit prepare dinner. It would be fun and keep her mind occupied. Inside, she found the post had come and left a letter for her from one of the design houses in New York, Ansell Harris. It enclosed a nice check and a list of questions that had Sheila frowning as she strolled into the kitchen, reading the letter.

"One of those, Miss Sheila," Bridgit grunted.

"One of what?" Sheila asked.

"One of those letters I call frowning letters. Neither good news nor bad news; just frowning news."

Sheila laughed. "They want to know a few things," she said. "Like whether I'm coming back or if I can send them designs from here. They say I owe them three more designs on my present contract, and they want to know whether I'm going to sign with them again or design for a rival firm."

"Well, it appears you've a good lot of decisions to make," Bridgit said.

"And those," Sheila said, her eyes darkening, "are the least of them. What's worse, Bridgit, I find I'm not able to make decisions. How can you make decisions when suddenly your whole world is changed, filled with unexpected problems and unexpected desires? How can you make decisions when you aren't sure what you want, or worse yet, aren't sure you can have what you want?"

"Are you perhaps referring to Mr. Brian?" Bridgit asked slyly. Sheila felt her cheeks coloring. She moved over to where the cook had set out her meat, chuck steak and neck of lamb.

"Maybe yes and maybe no," Sheila mused aloud, realizing they both knew the answer to that question. "These last seven years, Bridgit, I thought I had found what I wanted. I thought I had found myself. And then I began wondering about Connemara and thinking about coming back for a visit. Now that I'm here, I'm even more confused. It seems as though I'm still searching, now more than ever. Why, Bridgit, why? Most people don't have all this trouble finding themselves."

"No, that's true enough," the older woman remarked thoughtfully. "But then they haven't much to give, either."

"How do you mean that?" Sheila questioned.

"Well, it seems to me that finding yourself is somehow tied in with the giving of yourself," Bridgit went on. "Most folks are fairly simple. They eat, they sleep, they work and they make love, them that is lucky enough, that is. That's life for them, for most of us. But the ones like you, the sensitive ones, the creative ones, you have to give to the rest of us. But before you can give, you've got to come to terms with yourself, you've got to find yourself. As most of us have precious little to give, we have little trouble finding ourselves."

"Sometimes," Sheila said, "I wish there was some very wise person right here who could give us the answers to everything we asked. I'd have a lot to ask him."

"Well, now," Bridgit said, "that may not be the worst idea you've had. Have you paid the Witch o' Drumroe a visit?"

Sheila gasped aloud. The Witch o' Drumroe! She hadn't heard that name in so many years. Even when she was a little girl, it was a name one seldom brought up around Aunt Margaret. Aunt Margaret had no patience with talk of witches and their prophecies or their powers of clairvoyance. And as a little girl, Sheila had learned that before the death of her uncle, the Witch o' Drumroe had prophesied it. And now the cook had brought up that name from the past.

"The Witch of the Red Ridge," Sheila said aloud. "Don't tell me you believe in that old foolishness, Bridgit."

"I don't know if I believe or not," the woman answered honestly. "I know most folks pay attention to her. Most folks want no part of her, no part at all, and do you know why? Because she's been all too right in the past. What she's seen in her kettles and caldrons has come about all too often."

"I didn't think she was still living," Sheila said. "She was an old woman when I was a child."

"Some say she's not all that old," Bridgit said. "They say she only looks old because of the way she was treated, laughed at, called names, run away from. Maybe she is mad, I wouldn't know, but the mad have visions and powers denied to the rest of us."

Once, Sheila silently recalled, as a little girl, she had seen the Witch o' Drumroe in the woods on her way to the cabin on the Red Ridge where she lived. The red oaks had given the ridge its name, for when they shed in autumn the land was covered with a red blanket. Sheila recalled a crone-like figure, moving through the woods with surprising swiftness. Sheila also knew that Bridgit's words about the townsfolk were true; the people feared the woman they called a witch because of the many things she had prophesied correctly. Aunt Margaret, perhaps because of her own husband's death following one of the witch's prophecies, was particularly vehement about the "childishness" and "super-stition" connected with the woman she called a "poor demented creature."

"So you think a visit to the Witch o' Drumroe would help me find myself?" Sheila said, more lightly than she felt.

"I only know the woman has a way of seeing things," Bridgit answered. "Didn't she warn old Macahenny about an accident with a horse, and that week he rode to the hounds and was thrown and killed? Didn't she say she saw a great sickness, and they laughed at her and chased her out of town, and within two weeks the whole county was sick with the plague? Don't you know of these things, Miss Sheila?"

Sheila nodded, for in truth she did know of them; some she had heard as a youngster. And there were others she knew of. The Witch o' Drumroe had seen a great flame and in a week the old Killmore Manor House in East Drummfie had burned to the ground. Some said the old witch had set the fire herself to make her prophecy come true, but most professed only fearful belief in her. In a land where the banshees howl in the mists, where the wee folk gather in the moonlight, where the spirits of druids and pagan gods still live, where in St. Michan's Church in Dublin bodies lie in crypts for centuries without any sign of decay, in such a land it is little wonder that so many believe in the dark powers. Sheila felt a strange stirring, an uneasiness inside her as she thought about the Witch of the Red Ridge. Perhaps she should pay the old woman a visit. Of course, she was above taking anything like this seriously, but the old woman might know some old deep and dark secrets that could help her. And, she mused, warming to the thought, the old witch no doubt had a mountain of colorful outfits, capes and traditions she could borrow for her work. Yes, it might be fun, she told herself. She looked up to catch Bridgit studying her; the older woman broke into a laugh.

"Don't fret so on it, child," Bridgit said. "Whether you ever see the old witch or not, you'll be finding yourself one of these days. Just be patient and you'll come to it."

Sheila paused before she spoke, wondering how much she should confide in the woman about her fears and convictions. She decided against any revelation for the time being. She wouldn't involve another soul in this unless she had to do so.

"Bridgit, you're a comfort," Sheila said, impulsively hugging the older woman. "Come; let me help you with dinner. It's been a long time since I've seen one or had one, but the meat you've got there and that bag of potatoes, I'd make a guess you're going to make a Lancashire hot pot. Am I right?"

"Indeed you are, Miss Sheila." Bridgit beamed. "You can set everything out for me if you would. I like all my ingredients where I can get them before I start to cook."

"No sooner said than done," Sheila answered. And, making frequent trips to the cupboard, she brought out the potatoes, carrots, a large onion, lard, two stalks of celery, parsley, mixed herbs in a jar and salt and pepper. Bridgit set her to peeling and slicing the carrots, chopping the parsley, trimming and slicing the celery and the onion. Together, they placed the sliced potatoes at the bottom of a large brick-red casserole, then a layer of the diced meat over the potatoes and then alternate layers of mixed vegetables and meat, with the final top layer the remainder of the sliced potatoes.

"There!" Sheila exclaimed. "I do believe we've done it, and it looks beautiful. I'll leave the cooking of it to you."

"Thanks to you it went so quickly," Bridgit answered "I've plenty of time left to bake some soda bread. You go and rest or think about all those decisions you have to make."

Think! That was the last thing Sheila wanted time for now. There were too many thoughts she was trying to shut off for a little while at least. She stayed in the kitchen and helped the cook until it was time for her to change and get ready for dinner, grateful for the time-consuming business of her tasks.

Dinner was superb, and while she knew the Lancashire hot pot was Bridgit's doing, she felt a small, sneaking pride in it. She put off any talk of the attack until later, when the meal would be over. And so dinner, fortified by a bottle of Burgundy, a Chateau Lafite she had uncovered, was a happy, joyful interlude. Brian was at his most witty and charming and wrapped her in a blanket of happiness. When dinner was finally over, they strolled into the huge living room, already chilled by the night.

"I'll go and get a sweater," Sheila said.

"No," Brian answered. "Let me make a fire. Here; you sit down on the sofa."

He turned and knelt before the great fireplace, placing the logs on the iron supports, his head so ruggedly handsome, sturdy and strong. The flame from the first rush of the newly lighted fire illuminated his face and loosed a flood of memories upon Sheila, memories of all the fires Brian had lighted in that great fireplace, of all the wonderful moments they had spent together in that lovely room, on the very sofa she sat upon now. He knew, too. His small smile said so as he glanced up at her and came to sit down beside her. When he did, she had to hold herself back from leaning into his arms as she used to do. Maybe it was all the wine and good talk, she told herself, but she was feeling so warm and contented. Maybe, only she knew it was more than the wine, the fire and the dinner. It was Brian, that something about him that always made her feel so right by his side.

"I've been saving something to tell you," he said, his dark blue eyes twinkling. "The reading of the will has been set for tomorrow. Three in the afternoon, here at Doylan Hall. I've put everything in order and notified your cousin Grace and your great-uncle Regis Cluny. They'll be here. With you, there's no one else needed."

"I'm glad we're going to get it over with." Sheila grimaced. "I hate this kind of thing; it always makes me feel so morbid. And I've been saving something to tell you, Brian."

She sat up straight. Now she had to take up the terrible thing she had been pushing aside, on all the while that it could not be pushed aside. It was there, real and terrifying, and as she described what had happened the night before she relived every terrible moment of it. When she was finished she tried unsuccessfully to keep the triumph out of her voice.

"Now are you willing to believe me?" she asked. "Now do you still think Aunt Margaret was imagining things and that Terence just *ran away?*"

Brian got to his feet. His face was lined and severe, a furrow darkening his brows. He paced back and forth as though he were in a courtroom.

"There might be a connection between all these things," he said. "It's certainly a possibility we must face. But if we want to get at the truth, we must also face facts. Only facts, my girl, will help you find out what's true and what's not true. And facts are not something you like to deal with."

He paused as he saw Sheila's mouth open to answer, saw the temper start to flare in her eyes.

"Just hear me out," he said. "It's a fact that someone tried to attack you last night, probably to kill you. But all through your story to me you kept saying it was Bayliss who pursued you, yet you never saw the man who was after you. In truth it could have been anybody. It could have been a total stranger who saw you sleeping in the woods and followed you to attack you after dark. You were rather foolish to go up there alone if you feared Bayliss, and that's a fact, too."

"What about the hole in the fuel line of the Sunbeam?" Sheila snapped back. "Was that coincidental?"

"No, it was deliberate, but if Bayliss put it there while you were asleep as you claim, then anyone else could have done the same. Don't you see, Sheila, I'm just saying that accusing Bayliss doesn't make it a fact."

Sheila's anger cascaded inside her; she was made even more furious by the possibility that everything he said could be right. She hadn't seen anything but a shadowy figure, and yet she was certain of her convictions. He was just being the utter skeptic again, the lawyer. This time, though, she'd make him eat his skepticism.

"Facts, facts!" Sheila shot back at him. "Is that all you know about? As a lawyer, you certainly should know that facts aren't always the measure of truth. But if it's only facts you care about, I'll give you a few more. Didn't you tell me Bayliss has been doing odd jobs around the county? Handyman, driver, farmer's helper?"

"Yes, I said that."

"On the peat bogs, perhaps, cutting turf?"

"Yes, I happen to know he's been doing that."

Sheila strode from the room to return a moment later with the *slane*. She tossed it on the sofa before Brian.

"There's another fact," she exclaimed. "That *slane* was dropped by the man who tried to kill me last night. And a *slane* is used in cutting peat, now that's a fact, isn't it, Brian O'Donnell?"

She knew the sarcasm was dripping from her voice, but Brian merely held her blazing eyes with a cool, unwavering look.

"That is a fact," he agreed. "And it's also a fact that there isn't a man, woman or child in all of Connemara county who can't get hold of a *slane* or hasn't one of his own."

Sheila felt her cheeks grow red at the unqestionable truth of what he was saying.

"All right," she countered hotly, eyes flashing. "But Bayliss is the one who hated Aunt Margaret, Bayliss is the one who swore vengeance on her, Bayliss is the one who warned me to get out of Duncavan. Why are you so bent on defending him?"

"I'm not defending him or anybody, Sheila," Brian said, and Sheila heard his voice take on that dogged, stubborn note she knew so well. Maybe because it carried its own special brand of memories, maybe because it had always infuriated her, suddenly she was back seven years ago and her words were not so much words as echoes of the past she flung out at him.

"You're more than stubborn, Brian O'Donnell," she cried. "You're more than pigheaded. You're afraid to take a stand because you might be wrong, and you can't stand being wrong. You'd rather be safe than stick your neck out. You really haven't changed."

"And you're the same hotheaded, illogical, unreasoning creature," he said. "You don't listen. You're too busy shouting and being emotional to listen."

"You don't want me to listen; you want me to agree. That's all you wanted then, too," Sheila shouted. And with those words out of yesterday she knew they were no longer arguing about Bayliss but about something else, something that had never ended.

"That's not so," Brian retorted angrily. "I wanted the right thing for us then, and I do now!"

"For us?" Sheila said, her voice catching. She saw Brian step forward, saw his arms reach out and felt herself being pulled against his chest. Her lips lifted to his eagerly, hungrily, and all else, for the moment at least, was swept away by the sweet flood of his kisses.

"Sheila, Sheila," he murmured, "it's been so long."

"Too long," she answered between kisses. "But you didn't forget, either."

"Forget?" Brian said, stepped back and looked deep into her eyes. "How can one forget a sunbeam? How do you forget a rainbow? Besides, I'm not the forgetting kind. I never forget anything."

Sheila wanted to say: *Let's start over again, my love. Let's begin again, wiser and older and deeper.* But she didn't. He had kissed her, and she knew he still cared, but did he care enough to take up where they had left off? That she couldn't know yet, and suddenly she thought of a line from an old Kerry song she had learned many years ago:

> What would you do if the kettle boiled over?
> What would you do but set it again!

The kettle had boiled over seven years ago. Could she set it again? Time would answer that for her, she knew. Meanwhile, her own hopes and wants had to be put aside; they had to wait until this evil which covered her as a cloud covers the sun was put to an end. Pulling back from the safe circle of Brian's arms, Sheila said, "What are we going to do, Brian? I'm afraid. You're not convinced it's Bayliss. I am. But we do know someone tried to kill me last night, and I don't think it was a stranger passing through. I don't believe you think so, either. What are we going to do?"

"We're going to take every precaution we can," he said. "You're not to go anywhere without first telling Bridgit or me. Tomorrow, after the reading of the will, you might decide on further steps. A lot of things could change then. We can talk more about it tomorrow."

Sheila saw Brian to the door, where he kissed her lightly and she watched the red glow of the MG's taillights until they winked out of sight. Then she closed the door quickly, as the swirling mists brought back the night before. She hurried up to the warm comfort of her room, where she got into bed, lying awake in the dark, still feeling the sweet touch of Brian's lips on hers. There had been other arms around her these past seven years, but none of them had brought the warm haven that she had felt tonight. There was no escaping it any more: her love for Brian had never died. She had never been able to stamp it out, not with other arms or other lips. It had always been there inside her, always stressing the emptiness of her life without him, a subconscious reminder that she couldn't be happy without him. But what of Brian? she wondered. She had lived long enough and deeply enough to know that his kisses could have been nothing more than—she had to face it—*curiosity.* Or, without false modesty, she knew she was a highly attractive woman. His reactions to her could have been no more than normal masculine responses to a lovely woman. Oh, blast Sheila thought to herself. I'm getting like him, skeptical and doubting, analyzing the emotion out of everything. She turned on her side and closed her eyes. A weak moon filtered through the window. The answers she wanted would come in time, she was confident, the answers to this and to the evil that lurked somewhere outside. How could she know that those answers were so closely bound together?

Sheila was grateful for Brian's businesslike, professional approach the following afternoon at the reading of the will. He helped to depersonalize the entire proceedings, and the will itself seemed short and simple. Only when Terence was bequeathed a lifetime income from an annuity did she feel her hands grip the arms of the chair till they hurt. Her cousin, Grace Lyons, was left a large collection of expensive china she had always admired, plus a valuable collection of rare dolls. Uncle Regis Cluny was given the income from some rental properties in Cornwall, England. As Brian read on, his voice flat and measured, Sheila heard her name.

"To my niece, Sheila McCloud," he read, "I address this special message concerning Doylan Hall. I do not want Doylan Hall sold into the hands of strangers. This ancestral homes deserves better than that. It has given pleasure and security to generations, and yet a house is like a living thing to those who come to know it. It has its own character, its own personality. It should be a companion, not a chore; a friend, not a burden. I know that not everyone has the qualities to love a great house such as Doylan Hall, but I also know that Sheila McCloud has such qualities and such love to bring to it. And so I hereby bequeath Doylan Hall and all its physical contents not otherwise excepted herein to Sheila McCloud, with one provision, that being that it is her design and disposition to keep and to own Doylan Hall and to make it her home. Maintenance funds have been provided for this purpose.

In the event that such is not Sheila McCloud's wish and she rejects ownership of Doylan Hall, then it is to go to my faithful advisor and solicitor, Brian O'Donnell, whose assurances of proper maintenance and use I have been given."

Sheila sat back and closed her eyes. The remainder of the will was mostly legal technicalities and interested her little. So that was it. Doylan Hall was to be hers, but only if she wanted it. How very true to Aunt Margaret not to give an unwanted gift. She was humbled and touched and a little stunned. She hadn't expected the great house to be willed to her. She had expected her aunt to establish it as a show place perhaps, a period piece of its kind. But now as she thought upon it, she realized that would not be like Aunt Margaret, to put something she loved on exhibition. Finally, the reading completed, everyone left, and she was alone with Brian, who stood before her, briefcase in hand.

"Must you go?" she asked.

"Yes," he said. "This is something you must decide for yourself and by yourself. There is too much involved in it for you to let anyone influence you. Once you have reached your decision, firmly and finally, I'll help you all I can. I'll even tell you whether I think it was a good one or a poor one. But not now."

Sheila tried to read something in the dark blue eyes, but there was a curtain over them, almost as if, with the kisses of the night before, he had revealed something he was determined to keep hidden. She smiled inwardly. She had learned there were some things that would not stay hidden.

"I've got to go up to Linagh tomorrow," he said at the door. "I could stop by in the morning on my way if you like."

"I'd like that very much," Sheila said. "I'll have made my mind up by then, you can be sure. Come for breakfast, Brian."

He left then, and Sheila turned away. Slowly, as one would sip a fine brandy, she began to walk through every room of the great house. Some had not been used for years, and the furniture was covered with white linen sheets for protection, while others seemed to be waiting patiently for people to enjoy their strength and warmth. When she had walked the house from top to bottom, skipping only the cellar, she went to her room. She told Bridgit not to fix anything for dinner, that she wasn't hungry, and she pulled out the deep easy chair in the corner of the room to face the tall window and curled up in it. She could see the sun's glow faint in the sky over the moors and the cliffs at the edge of them. She let the dusk begin to gather in the room as she sat alone with her thoughts, pondering the decisions she must make. But was it really much of a decision? she asked herself. How many decisions are really made for us long before they come up? How often do we delude ourselves that we make decisions when all we do is to bow to what we knew all along? She did love this great house where she had grown up, where so much happiness once dwelled, where every weekend the halls rang to the sounds of music and laughter, to the thump of jigs and reels and polkas. She knew she would say yes, that she would accept, even though it might mean living there alone. That "decision," she smiled wryly to herself, had been easy enough to make. But what of the other decisions that were not hers alone to make? If Doylan Hall was to be hers, she wondered, would Brian also be hers?

It would be far simpler if she did refuse, if she returned to New York and her work, plunging herself into it with the same angry determination she had seven years ago. It might also free her from the spectre of death, a death which could well turn out to be her only real inheritance if she stayed on here. But she also knew that to run would be to return to another kind of emptiness. There would be no peace for her anywhere now, not until she knew whether Brian's love for her still burned as steadily, as unquenchably as hers did for him. As she wondered about that, she thought of Marla Culchane. Despite the venom of their meeting, despite the girl's warning to her, she had dismissed Marla as merely a warped and troubled soul. In that context, now, she had an understanding, no, an appreciation for the girl's inner turmoil. There was no peace for her, either, while she waited for Brian, while she was consumed with a thirst for vengeance. No, her staying here was a right thing, Sheila knew. It would clear away the still-smoldering debris of a fire that once had been, or it would send a renewed flame skyward with a purifying effect. Besides, there was still another factor that, even as she thought about it, sent her anger rising. To run, to refuse Doylan Hall, would mean closing the door not merely on a personal question but on Aunt Margaret's murder. It would mean leaving the monstrous evil free and untouched and unavenged, and that she would not do. Even if she had wanted to refuse Doylan Hall, she would have stayed on to find the killer. That was a debt she would pay for Aunt Margaret even if, and she drew her breath in sharply, it meant risking her own life again and again.

As she gazed out the window, the setting sun illumined the edge of a long cloud, forming a long red ridge across the sky. The red ridge seemed to grow in her eyes until Sheila could see nothing else and think of nothing else but the old woman, the Witch of the Red Ridge. She got up, as if a great invisible hand were pulling her. She had thought of the idea of visiting the old woman; had the sun-cloud formation been an omen of some kind, a sign for her to follow? Sheila took the Sunbeam out of the garage and headed for the heavily wooded land beyond Duncaven. If she were going to visit the old woman, this would be as good a time as any. It wasn't a far drive, and an old trail led up to the ridge itself. Once again she told herself she was disregarding ordinary reasoning to find out if the old woman knew anything that could help her track down the killer. She was a modern, sophisticated young woman, not a believer in witchcraft and the legendary hallucinations of old women. A small, persistent voice inside her kept whispering that as a modern, sophisticated young woman, she was aware of how little we know about the powers of the psyche and of the inner mind.

It was dusk and the night was gathering, but she had known that when she set out. Yet she was glad to reach the old foot trail below Red Ridge while it was still light. She had counted on that, too. She left the little car and walked quickly up the narrow path that grew steeper and steeper as she neared the ridge. In the half-light that was left, she managed to avoid low-hanging branches and protruding bushes. Reaching the ridge, she paused for breath, standing quietly among the tall trunks of the red oaks. Looking ahead through the trees, she saw the cabin, somewhat larger than she had imagined it would be, and began to walk toward it. A curl of smoke drifted lazily from a stone chimney, and as she neared, she saw the divided open pens alongside the small house, one for pigs, one for goats. Chickens and roosters strutted about freely. She saw only one cat, a large orange tom who moved casually across her path. She was disappointed. Weren't witches supposed to keep hordes of cats, black ones, too? The cabin was silent, and she halted outside it, wondering just what she should call out to the woman.

"Anybody home?" she tried, and immediately felt foolish. This wasn't visiting a neighbor. Only silence greeted her call.

"Hello," she called again, louder this time. Again there was no answer. She suddenly felt her skin tingling and had a strong feeling she was being watched. She didn't dare enter the cabin. There was something forbidding about its thick wooden walls, its small windows and the roof that sagged. She glanced around, growing more apprehensive by the minute. It was almost dark now, and then she saw the small urns placed in a semicircle, a wide arc, around the cabin. They stretched out to encircle the cabin halfway and were filled with some sort of fluid; at least the two nearest her were. The voice, when it came, frightened her so that she literally jumped as she whirled about.

"What do you want here?" the voice asked. Sheila gazed quickly about, and then she saw the figure standing between two of the giant oaks, as unmoving as the tree trunks beside her. It was the old woman, the Witch o' Drumroe, a long, cape-like garment hanging almost to her ankles, her hair, gray and stringy, framing her face. The woman detached herself from the trees and came forward, moving with long, powerful strides. As she did so, Sheila saw that her face was not so much sharp and cronelike as it was rawboned, with a gaunt, skeletal quality. The woman was tall, much taller than she had remembered.

"I came to see you," Sheila said, finding her voice. The woman stopped before the girl, and Sheila saw her eyes burned with a strange, inner glow, unlike any eyes she had ever seen before.

"Come inside," the woman said. It was a command, and Sheila followed her into the cabin. A huge iron caldron was being heated over a wide-mouthed fireplace, and two candles burned on a bench lining one wall. Trunks, boxes, bundles of clothes, kettles and pots, all tumbled in disarray, filled every corner of the cabin. A heavy rocker and two straight-backed chairs were the only pieces of furniture beside a round table. There was an adjoining room, Sheila saw, with the door half closed. A strange, somewhat bitter odor hung in the air, almost like an incense yet without the perfumed quality of incense. As she saw steam coming from the top of the huge iron caldron, Sheila concluded that the odor was coming from whatever was simmering inside the great kettle. The woman had turned to her and fastened those piercing eyes on her. Sheila felt as though she were being turned inside out.

"Why do you want to come see a madwoman?" the old woman asked. "You know who I am, and I know who you are.

I know everything that goes on around here. I sell my pigs and goats in the market, and I listen, that's all. It's not hard to listen. When no one talks to you, you get used to listening."

"I came because I thought perhaps you might know something which would help me," Sheila said, keeping her voice steady with an effort. "I've heard you know a lot of things about a lot of people. I'm prepared to pay you for any information you can give me. I'm interested mostly in a certain man, in whatever you might know about him."

The woman cut her off with a loud, startling cry that turned into a laugh, a high-pitched, derisive laugh that ended as abruptly as it had begun.

"You're lying!" the woman shot out, her lips flattening out against sharp, uneven teeth. "You came because they say I am a witch … the Witch o' Drumroe. You want more than scraps of gossip or bits of information. You want me to use my powers to see the things you cannot see. Well, I am not for hire. I only see what I see when it pleases me."

"I'm sorry I bothered you," Sheila said, feeling her heart pounding. The old woman was suddenly terribly frightening, her burning eyes now two coals of fire. She was indeed a madwoman and nothing else, Sheila concluded. All the rest was made up of coincidence and peasant superstition. She turned to go and saw, out of the corner of her eye, the woman's formless shape streak around the table and bar her way to the door.

"It's about the death of your aunt," the old woman said. "Yes, of course that's it."

The woman advanced toward her, and Sheila shrank back.

"You will stay," the woman commanded. "I will do this for you. Once, many years ago, this aunt of yours laughed at me. I was sorry for what happened afterward. I am always sorry when these things happen afterwards. I don't want to see the dark things, the terrible things. I want to see bright things, can you understand that?"

Sheila nodded, her throat too tight to speak. The woman seemed to yearn for a ray of understanding.

"Do you know the Mulloons in the valley?" she said, her voice eager. "No, you wouldn't. Well, they lived there for ten years without child. Then once I saw children for them, and in a year Mary Mulloon was with child. I saw happiness for the widow Brannigan, and an uncle left her a pot o' gold. Those are the things I want to see, but I can only see what's there, and they never remember anything but the black things. Never. Never."

Sheila watched as the woman went over to rummage amid the trunks and boxes, bringing forth a mason jar filled with dried mushrooms. She shot a glance at Sheila and mumbled aloud again.

"Only the bad they remember, only the bad," she intoned. "I'll see good for you if there's good to see. I'll do this for you."

In her own demented way she was attempting some sort of atonement, Sheila realized, for the prophecy which foretold her uncle's death. The girl found one of the straight-backed chairs and perched hesitantly on the edge of it, watching as the woman dropped three of the dried mushrooms in the caldron. Replacing the jar she beckoned Sheila to follow her into the next room. It was a smaller room, with a rumpled, dirty bed to one side and a heavy trunk against the other wall. The woman opened the trunk and Sheila stared down into it. The trunk was filled with a jumble of strange, dried, blackened and shriveled objects that at first were unrecognizable as anything in the semi-darkness. Then Sheila's eyes began to pick out the shriveled, curled tails of pigs and goats, the partly calcified hoofs and the dried tongues. She felt sick to her stomach.

You must choose one," the woman said. "Point to one."

Sheila pointed to a pair of hooves and turned away as the woman scooped them up, rushed out into the other room and dropped them into the caldron. Then, from another jar, she poured a thick, dark liquid into the kettle, which now steamed and bubbled vigorously. Sitting on the edge of the chair again, Sheila didn't dare to ask what the liquid was in the jar. The woman took up a burlap sack and poured a hail of acorns into the caldron. They were, Sheila saw, the shallow cupped acorns of the red oak, and almost at once the strange, bitter odor she had first smelled filled the room. Plainly it was caused by something in the acorns, the same substance in them which gave them their bitter flavor so disliked by squirrels, chipmunks and other animals. As Sheila watched, the woman picked up a piece of wood, lighted one end in the fire and with three swift, long strides crossed the cabin and rushed outside. There, Sheila saw her light the small urns, which flared up at once. In moments, the cabin glowed from the flaming semicircle of urns.

The woman returned and, leaving the door open, began to pace up and down the cabin floor, clenching and unclenching her hands. At each turn she would pause to look at Sheila with that penetrating glance, her eyes wild and deep in their sockets. She is mad, Sheila told herself, and I was mad to come here. She wanted to leave, to run, but fear held her there. The woman was worked up now. There was no telling what she might do if Sheila decided to flee. Those long, powerful strides could overtake her in seconds. No, she had to wait, and hope the moment would pass without incident.

Suddenly the woman stopped, took a large pewter cup from the mantel atop the fireplace, plunged it into the caldron and scooped up the bubbling concoction. She held it over her head in a devotional gesture, stirred the cup and then drank it in one long, unbroken swallow. She put the cup back on the mantel, walked to the rocker and sat down facing Sheila, her eyes focused on the girl in a wide-eyed stare. For minutes she sat transfixed, staring at the girl, and Sheila began to wonder if the woman was not in some sort of trance. Then she began to moan, softly at first, then louder. As she closed her staring eyes, she began to cry out.

"I see," she wailed. "I see colors, I see light, I see the sky. It is all coming together."

Sheila had heard of hallucinations caused by herbs, roots, fungi. Was this the secret of the woman's witchcraft, merely visions resulting from natural drugs? Or was this the way in which she freed her psychic powers, opening up the inner eye?

"I see, I see," the woman continued to moan with eyes tightly shut. Sheila swallowed and forced herself to speak.

"What do you see?" she asked fearfully.

"I see, I see," the woman continued again, and then she sat straight up in the rocker, her eyes snapping open wide in a sightless stare. "I see *death*!" She screamed the last word.

"Where do you see death?" Sheila breathed, leaning forward. "Whom do you see?"

"Yes, yes," the woman moaned. "I see it, I see it. I see death, and there is a woman ... no, there are two women. Yes, there are two women, and death is reaching out for one of them."

Sheila's heart froze. Two women, one to be touched by death's icy fingers. Two women, she gasped as her mind flew to Marla Culchane's venomous warning. No, no, she said aloud, shaking her head vigorously. It just couldn't be Marla Culchane. The old hag was nothing but a wild, half-crazed creature and her visions nothing but wild hallucinations. The old woman had closed her eyes again and begun to wail, a pitiful, heart-rending wail that rose and fell in a steady pattern. She sat there, eyes tightly shut again, rocking back and forth and wailing. Sheila leaped to her feet and ran headlong out the door, through the spaces between the flaming urns and along the Red Ridge. As she reached the steep trail from the ridge, she looked back. The witch's wails resounded through the night, echoing among the great red oaks, and the cabin glowed and flickered by the light of the flaming urns, a fiery necklace encircling the front of the house. It was a scene she would not soon forget, Sheila knew as she ran down the trail, grateful for the distance which finally swallowed up the woman's wails. She leaped into the car and roared off back down the road, realizing her body was wet with perspiration and her stomach churning.

It wasn't till she was back in her room at Doylan Hall that her stomach began to stop its whirling, throbbing gyrations. She undressed and crawled under the covers, but she could not shut out the scene or the woman's words. She tried to summon all her powers of dispassionate reason. Nothing, she told herself sternly, had really happened to change her decisions made earlier that day. She would accept Doylan Hall and hope for Brian's love. She would accept Doylan Hall and continue to bend every minute of the day to one thing: tracking down and exposing Aunt Margaret's killer. All that remained unchanged, unswerving. The old woman's words could be nothing but pure wild imaginings, she knew. And yet she also knew how often the woman had been uncannily right in the past. Most of all, she was shaken by the entirely unexpected quality of the woman's vision. Two women, with death reaching out for one. It had been no woman who had pursued her through the Dolmens. And she doubted it had been a woman behind Terence's abduction. Yet as she thought about it, one nagging, chilling possibility refused to be set aside. What if her attempted killer was a hired assassin? It was an all too possible conclusion. But there were so many aspects that defied understanding if Marla was indeed involved. Sheila could understand the girl's hatred of her, even to the twisted, warped desire to eliminate her. But where did this fit into Aunt Margaret's murder? It just didn't hang together unless, and here Sheila's mind held fast, there was more sickness in Marla Culchane than anyone suspected. If so, Sheila had to find out for herself if she could, and there was but one way to do that ... meet with the girl again. She would do it, Sheila decided. She would do it tomorrow. She was confident that with another meeting, she would know whether to dismiss the witch's words or pay more heed to them.

Suddenly, so suddenly she leaped up in bed, a brilliant flash tore the night apart, followed by an ear-shattering clap of thunder. She had been so absorbed in her thoughts she hadn't noticed the wind had grown fierce enough to rattle the shutters. Now another thunderclap shook the windows, and Sheila crept lower under the covers. The sound of rain driving hard against the windowpanes signaled the storm breaking over the great house. She finally went to sleep, not realizing that the storm was but the harbinger of another kind of storm that would soon break over her.

CHAPTER SEVEN

Bridgit had made pancakes with rashers and biscuits with jam for breakfast, and in between mouthfuls, Sheila told Brian her decision.

"I'm glad, he said. "About the first part of it, anyway."

"What does that mean?" Sheila asked defensively.

"It means I'm happy you are going to stay here and become mistress of Doylan Hall. I'm unhappy about your wanting to pursue ghosts out of the past."

Not pursue ghosts out of the past? Sheila wondered what he meant by those words. Did he also mean not to pursue the ghosts of their love? Her reply was tart.

"It would seem that the ghosts are pursuing me," she snapped. "And very live ghosts they are, too!"

Brian had finished his coffee and stood up, his face set, impassive, his words reflecting controlled anger. Nonetheless, they carried a shaft of sunlight in them.

"Must you always be so difficult, Sheila McCloud?" he asked. "Must you always make it so hard for those who want only the best for you?"

"I don't want to be difficult," Sheila answered. "But this is a cloud I must lift for Aunt Margaret, for Doylan Hall, for myself and, in truth, for all of Duncavan."

"God, girl," Brian shot back, "let Duncavan take care of itself. If there is a murderer about, he'll expose himself again without your risking your life to catch him."

"No, not this murderer," Sheila said. "Aunt Margaret had found out something about him, and unless I find out what that was he may never be caught. And I could never be happy here knowing that her killer was walking around scot free. I shouldn't think you'd want that, either."

"Of course I wouldn't," Brian said. "But I don't want you getting killed, either. If that attack on you wasn't an isolated thing, if this all does tie together somehow, then you certainly are in danger. But if the killer gets the idea that you are dropping the whole thing, then the danger to you may well vanish."

"And he might, too," Sheila said. "If coming after me will make him reveal himself, then that's a risk I'll have to take. Besides, I'm thinking it's too late to stop now."

She said nothing at all of her visit to the Witch o' Drumroe or of the woman's vision. There would be time for that after she visited Marla. Brian's hands found her shoulders, and his eyes bored deeply into hers. He shook his head slowly.

"What am I going to do with you?" he said, more a statement than a question. "I'll pass back this way tonight, sometime after dinner. I'll stop in then. Meanwhile, you're not to go anywhere without telling Bridgit."

Happy at the concern in his voice and his words, Sheila watched him drive off and then, flinging a jacket over a cream-colored silk blouse and a skirt of violet heather, hurried to get the car.

"I'll be in Duncavan," she flung back at Bridgit in the kitchen. "I'm going to visit Marla Culchane."

As she imagined, the Culchane house was still the same, standing on the corner of Paul Street midway into town. Mrs Culchane, looking considerably aged, had answered the door. She was polite but cold and went to call Marla down at once. Sheila waited in a small foyer just inside the door, and when Marla appeared Sheila forced a gay, bright smile. The other girl, wearing a pink shirt-waist dress, would have been more than attractive if the lines around her mouth had not been so hard and set.

"Hello, Marla," Sheila exclaimed brightly. "I've stopped by to have a little talk with you. I think it's in order."

Marla Culchane's eyes made a short tour of Sheila's outfit and then lapsed into sullenness.

"I've said all I have to say to you," she commented.

"Can't we be friends, Marla?" Sheila began again. "Can't we let bygones be bygones?"

"Just like that, now," the other girl said, her eyes icy with dis-dain. "How easy for you. Just come back from America, very suc-cessful, very independent, *the* Miss Sheila McCloud, graciously willing to forgive and forget. My, my but that's big of you."

"That's not it at all," Sheila said. "I hoped we could be friends, really I did."

"And you're not here with your cap all set for Brian O'Donnell? Don't tell me that lie."

The girl was filled with bitterness, so much so that it exuded from her, filling the room with hate. But Sheila felt her own tem-per rising.

"I didn't come to tell you any lies," she said. "But really, Marla, you can't hold your own failures against me. After all, I've been gone for seven years. That should have been ample time for you to make Brian forget me, don't you think?"

"Oh, indeed, if you really had been gone. But you weren't gone ... not ever, ... not seven years, not seven weeks, not seven days."

"How can you say that?" Sheila protested.

"Easily, because it's true. You took your body away, but you stayed here in a hundred different ways. Everytime he'd go to the end of town there you'd be, standing atop the hill. Don't laugh. Doylan Hall was you, an everyday reminder of you. I used to watch him stand and look up at the place, and I could see what he was thinking. Then there was Lady Margaret, making Brian solicitor for her so she'd be in constant touch with him. She saw to it that he was kept fully informed of your activities in America. There was always a letter or two she'd tell him about. I used to ask at parties where we'd meet whether he heard from you, and he always had something to tell me from some letter Lady Margaret had read him. You gone away? Why, you might just as well have been right here in Duncavan."

Sheila's mind raced. It was clear the girl hated Lady Margaret, too. She blamed her aunt for keeping a memory constantly alive in Brian's heart, a memory that, if left to fade away, would have given her a chance. Perhaps the old witch had been right: there were two women, one touched by death, Marla and herself. Or perhaps, as Brian had put it, the girl hated everybody. But she had heard enough to send cold fingers reaching up and down her spine. The old woman's vision and the girl's intense hatred were more than she could dismiss. She turned away and opened the door to go.

"I'm staying," she said quietly. "I'm staying until I find the answers I'm looking for ... all of them."

"We'll see," Marla called after her. "We'll see."

Sheila went back to Doylan Hall. She had been so certain it was Bayliss. It could still be Bayliss was the actual killer, but now she saw him as perhaps no more than a tool for Marla Culchane. How deep did the girl's hate and vindictiveness go? How far had it distorted and twisted her mind? Deep enough to do what had been one? But what of Aunt Margaret's letters? They had spoken of "something monstrous" here in Duncavan. Could this be what she had meant, a monstrous sickness? Somehow it didn't come out right, and yet there was the old woman's vision ... two women and the spectre of death ... Marla Culchane and herself. Sheila paced her room angrily, upset and confused. It was just too impossible to believe, she told herself. Marla's hate couldn't be that deep, couldn't lead to murder. Once again she knew that the only answer to it all would be to uncover what Lady Margaret had learned, to retrace her aunt's steps until they led her to the same place.

She changed to a lime blouse and dungarees and hurried downstairs to the library and the task of going through each book. One of them could contain a note, a slip of paper, some hidden clue that could supply the missing pieces. Sheila began to pull out the books one by one, holding each one face down and vigorously shaking it. By late afternoon she had amassed a small pile of old letters, notes, bookmarks, pressed flowers, shopping lists and other unimportant scraps. With a dejected sign and aching arms, she put the last volume back into its place on the bottom shelf. She went back to her room, delved under the blouses and sweaters and took out the two old newspapers. She sat there spreading them out on the bed, scanning their faintly yellowed pages. Once more they said nothing to her.

"The old safe in the study is next." She sighed tiredly. Tom Grogan in Duncavan would have the equipment to pry open the heavy doors, and she was on her way to pick up the phone when she heard the doorbell ring and Bridgit talking to someone. Sheila waited, and a moment later Bridgit appeared.

"It's Mr. Harry Glendon to see you, Mum," she said. "He's come callin'."

"Please show him in," Sheila said. She greeted the man as he came into the library with hesitant, shy steps. His tall, spare frame was slightly stooped, and once again she was impressed by the deep weariness of his eyes, eyes which spoke of an inner pain and grief. They seemed to reflect, from their dark orbs, some inner desolation that had been long and silently borne. He seemed somewhat ill at ease in her presence.

"Please excuse the dungarees," Sheila said brightly. "Please sit down. Would you like some tea?"

"That would be lovely if it's not an imposition," Harry Glendon said as Sheila motioned to Bridgit. "I was just walking nearby and hoped you'd be in. You know, I've wanted so to come by to visit you. I feel a special closeness to you, my dear, for many reasons."

As they sipped the tea which Bridgit quickly brought, the man appeared to relax, and his tenseness subsided. Only the sadness in his eyes remained constant.

"First," he went on, "you no doubt have heard that your aunt's tragic death was a terrible echo for me. It brought back all the anguish of finding poor Nora in almost the exact same spot. I tell you, my dear, when I heard about Lady Margaret, it was like living a horrible experience all over again. I can't tell you how upset I was. I didn't go out of my cottage for days. We had become rather good friends, Lady Margaret and I, I'm proud to say. We used to meet regularly on our respective walks across the moors. In fact, Lady Margaret and I had been discussing a business project I am contemplating. Nothing big, but it was something she was interested in investing in with me. Yes, my dear, she was a fine woman, a fine woman."

Harry Glendon paused and sat silent, caught up in memories of his own, captured by private thoughts for an instant. Then, when he suddenly returned his attention to her, his words took Sheila by complete surprise.

"Have you found anything further, my dear?" he asked, leaning forward and speaking softly. "Lady Margaret was upset, you know, or hadn't she told you?"

Sheila's heart leaped. Apparently Aunt Margaret had confided in this hollow-eyed, soft-spoken man. But what had she told him? Could he provide her with additional pieces?

"She wrote me she was afraid of something," Sheila said, "something and someone. I believe I know who it was she feared, but I must have more proof, more real evidence, before I can do anything about it. What had she told you, Mr. Glendon? Did she ever mention a name, a man called Bayliss?"

"Bayliss ... Bayliss." Harry Glendon frowned thoughtfully. "Isn't he the chap she had that trouble with some while back? He used to work for her or something like that?"

"The same," Sheila said. "Did she tell you she was afraid of him and why?"

"No," the man said. "I only know she was afraid of something. That much she had told me, and she was going to tell me more when it happened. Of course, I thought then that it was a horrible accident just as poor Nora's was. I don't know that it wasn't, but I got to thinking about Lady Margaret being afraid, and so I had to come and talk to you. She often spoke about you, her very successful niece in America, and I knew if there was anyone she would have confided in, it was you."

"Unfortunately, she only wrote enough for me to be convinced it wasn't an accident, Mr. Glendon," Sheila said. "And I won't rest until I find out the truth."

"Well, now, my dear," Harry Glendon said, "I want to help in any way I can. It will be my way of repaying Lady Margaret's many kindnesses to me. Perhaps if we put our heads together, we can come up with something. You tell me about anything you come across, and I'll go home and keep thinking if there is anything I can remember that might help."

"Oh, do, please do," the girl exclaimed excitedly. "And if you think of anything, please call me at once. I do appreciate what you're doing so much."

"Nonsense," he disclaimed. "You can count on my help at any time, any time at all, night or day. You just call me whenever you like. Or, better still, come drop by to see me. I'm in the cottage on the other side of the moors, just past the thatch of shrubs on the Skerry Road. You can't miss it."

Harry Glendon stood up, his round, deep eyes if anything a little sadder, his shoulders perhaps a trifle more stooped.

"Then we'll keep in touch, Miss McCloud, and thank you for the tea."

When he left Sheila's heart was lighter. She had not only found an unexpected friend and ally in her search, but Harry Glendon's words vindicated her conclusions. Aunt Margaret had spoken to someone else of her fears. But it had grown too late to have Tom Grogan come and open the old safe, so she put that off till the morning. Instead, Sheila sat down to answer her letter from New York and to dash off a few lines to some friends. She wrote Harris Ansell that she would have the three designs for them soon and of her plans to continue designing for them but to work out of Duncavan. As she described how she would be making frequent trips to Paris, London, Rome and New York, and how it would actually be more convenient for her to work out of Doylan Hall, she kept hearing a voice from the past, Brian's voice, telling her the very same things she was now setting down on paper. She had just finished when she heard Brian's voice again, this time filling the hallway downstairs, and she raced down to tell him of Harry Glendon's visit.

"I guess that proves it once and for all," she said when she'd finished.

"Proves what?" Brian asked quietly.

"That Aunt Margaret was afraid of something. I'm not the only one she told it to."

"I never said she wasn't afraid," Brian answered. "I only said her fears might have been imaginary things."

Seeing the angry protest leap into her eyes, he put his finger over her lips and pulled her into his arms, his eyes soft and kind, smiling down at her.

"Don't start," he said. "I've been thinking about you as I drove back, and I think you need a change of atmosphere. I want you to get away for a day. You've been living with this ever since you returned to Duncavan. The Sunbeam is fixed; take a day's outing for yourself. Take the long drive to Galway; it'll do you good."

"I was going to have Tom Grogan open the old safe in the morning," Sheila thought aloud.

"It can wait another day. You need to get away," Brian said. "You need the relaxation."

The long drive to Galway, Sheila thought. She could take the scenic coastal road through Bally-conneel, Cashel and Inveran and along the edge of lovely Galway Bay. It would be fun. It might clear her mind so it could think better, too.

"Maybe you're right," she mused.

"I know I'm right," Brian said. "Start out bright and early tomorrow morning, and take your time. I'm sorry I can't go with you, but I'll know where you've gone, and you'll be away from here. The important thing is for you to have a nice, relaxing day, and I'll see you when you get back in the evening."

"All right!" Sheila decided. "I'll do it." Brian's kiss was hurried but tender and sweet nonetheless, and that night the girl went to bed without her heart pounding and her mind whirling for a change. Hidden death seemed to hang less heavily in the air as she closed her eyes, soon slipping off into the regular breathing of deep sleep. The venerable old grandfather's clock in the corner of the room said three A.M. when she sat bolt upright, a half-scream escaping her lips, her body shaking and wet with a cold perspiration. But she was alone, she quickly saw, and she forced her trembling limbs to hold still. She must have had a nightmare that had frightened her into waking. Yet she had no recollection of one. But she didn't know; did one always know about night-mares? There had been no strange noise that had wakened her. It had to have been a nightmare to leave her so wet and shaking. What else except ... and Sheila felt her throat tighten ... except a premonition, an omen from the unknown, a cry of warning from some primordial instinct. Oh, dear God, Sheila murmured, fall-ing back onto the pillow. Brian was so right; she had to get away for a day. In a while her breath grew more regular again, and she lapsed back into sleep while the night ticked itself away until the sun fought its way through the dawn.

Sheila was in the kitchen at breakfast when she told Bridgit of her plan for the day. The cook looked dismayed for a moment. "Oh, Mum," she said, "I'm fresh out of cleaning wax, and I'd planned to do the living room today. It's a fair day's job, you know. Can you give me ten minutes to take the car and run into town and back? That's all it'll take: ten minutes."

"Of course, Bridgit," Sheila answered. "And don't race down and back. I'm not in any special hurry. I can wait."

"It's good of you, Miss Sheila," the older woman said, whip-ping off her apron and hurrying out the door. Sheila poured herself a third cup of tea and began to look through the morning journal. She had just spread a generous helping of jam on a biscuit when she heard a loud, thunderous crash and Bridgit's voice, a cry of pain suddenly cut off. Sheila raced outside, stifling her own scream with the back of her hand as she saw the woman's figure lying in the garage doorway, crumpled under the weight of a heavy oak beam. As she ran over to where Bridgit lay unmoving she saw, in horror, the wet red pool forming by the woman's temple. The heavy oak beam had formed the lintel above the double doors, and while it still hung by one end, the other part lay across Bridgit's body. Using strength summoned from some unknown source, Sheila managed to push the beam to one side and then run into the house to phone Constable Connaughten. She told him they would need an ambulance and then, with a pan of warm water and a washcloth, she hurried back to where the unconscious woman lay. She knelt beside Bridgit and bathed her head with the warm water as she tried to stem the flow of blood.

"Bridgit, can you hear me?" Sheila asked, smoothing the gray hair back from the woman's face. Bridgit had, in a short time, become not just a cook, not just a servant, but a comfort, an object of stability. There was no hospital as such in Duncavan, and Constable Connaughten and an aide arrived first to wait the ambulance from Clifden. It came surprisingly quickly, and as they gently put Bridgit into the white vehicle with its flashing red lights, Sheila spoke to Constable Connaughten.

"I guess no one has really checked those old garage doors for a long time," she said. "We had a bad thunderstorm the other night, and the rain probably finished sweeping away rotted wood. Anyway, when Bridgit opened the doors, the lintel gave way and fell."

"Come on, Miss McCloud," the policeman said. "You ride with me."

With a roar and the whine of sirens, the two cars sped down the country roads at breath-taking speed.

"Do you think …" Sheila began the dread question and then left it unfinished. "If only she'd moan or something."

"She's had a bad one," the constable said. "But we'll be at the hospital in a few minutes, and they'll be giving you more information then."

The hospital itself, small but modern, was reassuring in its quiet efficiency. Sheila was ushered into a small, cool-hued waiting room, and she was grateful to the police chief for not trying to make small talk. A doctor finally appeared, an information form in his hand.

"There's no need to bother you with a lot of questions," he said. "The identification in Bridgit's billfold has given us all the important data we need on her. She has, I'm afraid, a severe skull fracture."

"She'll be all right, won't she?" Sheila hopefully phrased the question.

"I can't say," the doctor said gently. "I'd like to be more encouraging, but it would be dishonest. She may not live, Miss McCloud. It will be touch and go. We'll call you as soon as there is any change in her condition. Right now she is in a deep coma."

Sheila felt Constable Connaughten's hand at her elbow, felt his steady touch guiding her to the waiting car. It was only when they were back in Duncavan that he spoke to her.

"Shall I take you back to Doylan Hall, Miss McCloud?" he asked her.

"No, thank you, Constable," Sheila said. "I want to walk a little. You've been very kind."

"Accidents will happen," the police officer said. "That's why they are called accidents. They are nobody's fault."

Sheila's eyes expressed her gratitude at his words of kindness, and she waved as the car drove off. She turned and headed for Brian's office.

"Sheila!" he exclaimed as she walked in, half-rising from his chair, a frown of complete surprise on his face. "What are you doing here? I thought you were on your way to Galway long ago!"

Unable to hold back the tears any longer, she fell into his arms and sobbed out what had happened. Brian produced a bottle of whiskey from a desk drawer and poured a tumbler out for her. It was warm and strengthening as it went down her dry throat.

"I'll drive you home," he said. "I've someone coming, but they can wait."

"No," she refused. "I want to walk. I need the air. I just had to stop by and see you for a minute."

"I'll be over tonight, then," he said. "You go home and take it easy. You've had a bad shock."

Sheila walked down Creighton Street to where it ended at Father Thomaseen's. In the quiet dark of the church, she lit a candle for Bridgit and knelt before it in silent prayer. Then she walked home, a terrible heaviness in her heart. Brian had said to take it easy, but she couldn't lie around and have all that time to think and to sit in despondency. She had to keep busy, to work. She changed into dungarees and a sweater, took a long-handled broom, a mop and a bucket of water and suds and marched back to the garage to clean up the debris. In falling, the heavy lintel had pulled down years of small splinters and encrusted dirt and bits of wood. With the broom, Sheila knocked down the remaining loose bits and pieces. After washing away the ugly stain, she went over to where the heavy beam still hung by one end, deciding that the first thing would be to try to pull it down completely.

The girl grasped the loose end that had fallen with her hands, and as she did so she glanced down at it to avoid running splinters into her hands from the broken edge. But what she saw made her heart leap. There was no splintered edge, no jagged end to the beam. It was neat and clean, the straight edge of a beam that had been sawed. As she stared at it, the realization of what she saw before her rose up like some hideous apparition suddenly loosed from its cave. The lintel had not just been torn away, weakened by wear and weather. One end had been sawed through so that when the garage doors were opened it would dislodge and fall, just as it had done. She ran her hand over the clean, sharp edge, as if to let her fingers corroborate what her eyes had seen. It had been no accident, no accident at all! And it hadn't been meant for Bridgit. Poor Bridgit had been merely an innocent victim, the proverbial bystander. It had been planned to kill her, Sheila realized, a cold hand gripping her heart. The heavy lintel had been meant for her, to crash down upon her head as she opened the garage doors. She would normally have been the one to do so, and one more tragic "accident" would have occurred at Doylan Hall.

And now she saw something else clearly. The Witch o' Drumroe flashed before her eyes. The woman's vision had been so very right. She had "seen" two women and death reaching out for one; only the two women had not been she and Marla Culchane but she and poor Bridgit! Sheila swayed in the sunlight, feeling lightheaded and faint, and reached out a hand to steady herself against the garage wall. As she trembled at the realization of how close to death she had again come, she also knew that her fears and suspicions regarding Marla were a false trail. The old woman's vision, right as it had been in its basic prophecy, had led her down the wrong path insofar as Marla Culchane was concerned. True, Marla hated her, but that hate, as Brian had said, was only part of the inwardly turned, all-consuming bitterness of the girl. Sheila knew that she faced a killer who was acting out of desperate necessity, not out of vindictiveness or unrequited love. The killer she faced was a determined murderer who clearly feared what she might uncover if she persisted.

Sheila swallowed and straightened up. Other inescapable conclusions flooded in on her like a frightening torrent. The killer had struck again, and he would continue to strike. How long could she be this lucky? He would soon learn, if indeed he hadn't found out already, that he had missed again. News of the "accident" at Doylan Hall would be all over Duncavan by this time. He would know that now she was going to be alone in the great house. She saw deep black eyes and unruly black hair, a face cunningly planning his next move. Would he come after her in the house, perhaps that night? She told herself she couldn't think about such things, and yet she knew she had to. She cast about for something reassuring, some hopeful straws to cling to in a sea of fear. And without stretching logic out of shape, she found something. The killer was still trying to create "accidents." That meant he had to plan each step with caution. So far he had been successful, diabolically successful, in making everything that happened appear unplanned. To do otherwise could be dangerous. To kill her within the safe walls of Dovlan Hall might arouse suspicion. He obviously still wanted whatever happened to appear to be accidental, but she couldn't be sure how important it still was to him. Something was making him bolder, more desperate. Probably it was the fear that the longer she lived, the closer she might come to uncovering what Aunt Margaret had found. Bayliss, she told herself, had to be the one. He had stolen into the garage last night with a saw, and she recalled waking with a cold fright. Some inner sense had indeed tried to warn her that death was prowling close by in the night.

Her mind whirling, Sheila took the broom and began mechanically to sweep up the debris on the garage floor. She would ask Brian to stay at Doylan Hall tonight. At least then she wouldn't be alone. She gave a short, almost harsh laugh as she recalled how often, as a child and then a young girl, she would revel in having the great house to herself when Aunt Margaret and the servants were all away for a spell. And now she was filled with utter dread at the thought of having to be alone within its walls. As she swept the debris into a neat pile, something amid the wood splinters, dust and dried leaves rolled off to the side. Bending over, she picked up the small, round object and saw it was a button, a button from the sleeve of a man's jacket. Medium gray, flecked with brown markings, it was distinctive. Sheila closed her fist tightly around it, her heart leaping with the importance of what she had found.

She was already wondering how to find out where Bayliss was living. If she could go through his things, find the jacket with the button missing, she'd have him trapped and with more than enough evidence to bring him before the police. It would definitely place him inside the garage last night, and the sawed-through edge of the lintel would complete the picture. She thrust the button into the pocket of her dungarees and ran back into the house. She phoned Brian, only to hear the voice of the operator he employed to take calls when he was out of the office. "Mr. O'Donnell has gore to Antrim for the afternoon," she said. "He'll be back by early evening, miss."

Sheila put down the phone, her lips set and thin. No matter. She wouldn't wait; she couldn't. This was far too important. Besides, it was still morning, and Bayliss was likely to be at whatever work he was doing. If she were to go through his things, it would have to be when he was away. Quickly she dialed another number and was relieved to hear a soft, gentle voice answer.

"It's Sheila McCloud, Mr. Glendon," the girl said. "I want to ask a favor of you."

"Oh, my dear, of course," the man said. "I was thinking of calling you. I've just come back from Duncavan, where I heard about the accident at Doylan Hall. How positively terrible!"

"Thank you," Sheila said, envisioning the concern in those deep, dark eyes. "That's why I'm calling, as a matter of fact. It wasn't an accident, Mr. Glendon. I don't want to go into the whole thing now, but believe me, it was no accident. I must find out where this man Bayliss is living. I've got to go through his things. Do you know where he is, or can you find out?"

There was a long pause, and then Harry Glendon said, "Bayliss, eh? Well, my dear, mightn't that not be dangerous to do?"

"Not if he's off at work somewhere and I can get in," Sheila said. "I must try, anyway. It's terribly important. I found something I think could trap him once and for all."

"All right," the man said. "Linus Rearden at Malachy's Tobacco Store always seems to know everything about everybody. Maybe he can help me. I'll call you back in a little while, my dear."

Sheila put the phone down, feeling less alone. Harry Glendon was helping her and Brian would surely stay the night if she asked him. She decided to stay in her dungarees. She might find it necessary to climb through a window, and a dress would only be hindrance. She took the button from her pocket and examined it again, imprinting its medium gray and brown flecked markings on her mind. Then she put it into her bureau drawer. She wouldn't take it along and risk losing it. She'd know its companions when she saw them, without question. Only ten or fifteen minutes had passed, but it seemed like hours, when the phone rang insistently.

"I think I've some information for you," Harry Glendon said. 'It's the best I could do, my dear. Bayliss was last living in Multyowen and working on a farm about five miles from there. You know anything about Multyowen and where it is?"

"I do, Mr. Glendon," Sheila said, excitement in her voice. "You wouldn't have found out where in Multyowen he lives, would you?"

"Only that it was in one of the flats," the man said. "Now you be careful, my dear, won't you?"

Sheila quickly agreed to be cautious and turned from the phone to half-run out to the garage. Multyowen, was it? she mused. It was, she remembered, a dirty little town on the way to Sligo, about an hour's drive. The name itself meant River Mills, and a large mill and fabric company had just opened a new plant there, virtually building the town for the mill, when she had taken leave of Connemara seven years ago. She searched her memory, seeming to recall a letter once from her aunt which said the mill had failed and the town was now used mostly as a lower-class boarding house for transient and itinerant work-men who lived in the "flats," the rows of four-story tenements that the mill had erected for its workers. Driving down the road through Duncavan in the Sunbeam, she grimaced as she thought of Multyowen and the task ahead of her. But it would be well worth it. It would be about one or two in the afternoon when she reached the town. If Bayliss still worked on a farm five miles out, he'd probably be ending work about four. That would give her two hours to find his flat and go through it ... if she could get in. It would be enough time with a little luck, and she knew she'd be needing luck. It wouldn't be exactly like finding a needle in a haystack, but it could be enough of a task.

The girl drove fast, wishing the huge super-highways of America might, for the moment, magically replace the pictur-esque but slow roads of Ireland. The wonderful, lilting name on markers flashed by the speeding car: Killavally, Castlebar, Tobercurry, Drumfin. Finally she turned off at a dirty, smudged sign that said "Multyowen." It was a proper introduction to the town, grim, grimy and really not much more than a few streets in between the rows of narrow, ugly buildings that adjoined one another. She had seen towns like this before; they existed in plen-tiful profusion up north around Belfast and in the industrial sections of Wales and England. But there, at least, they had the saving grace of life, of movement and action, of a certain sooty vitality of their own. But Multyowen was not more than an echo of a mill town, a place where men lived while they were marking time on their way to some place better. She parked the Sunbeam at the first row of the tenement flats and began her search, first examining the doorbells and mailbox names in each dim, dingy hallway.

It was slow work, and she could only hope that the torn and empty name slots were really without tenants. Sheila began to grow apprehensive as time raced on and she was not even half-way through the buildings. A few idlers and one rawboned land-lady had stared at her curiously, and now she was glad she had stayed in her dungarees, for they were less out of place here. She had about reached the halfway mark in her search of the flats when she saw it, a handwritten bit of paper stuck into the name plate in the hallway: *Bayliss—3*.

"Who you lookin' for, lady?" the voice behind her asked, and Sheila jumped. She whirled to see a boy, about ten years old but with the hard-bitten, wizened face of a youngster who had grown wise far beyond his years on the streets. His torn jacket was opened and the shirt beneath it dirty and frayed, and Sheila saw he regarded her with skeptical eyes that were ready to disbe-lieve anything they were told.

"You live here?" Sheila asked, trying to sound calm.

"Around," he said flatly.

"I was looking for Mr. Bayliss," Sheila said. "Do you know him?"

"He ain't home yet," the urchin answered. Sheila made her-self look dismayed. She was here, and time was getting short. She had to plunge on, recklessly or not.

"He has something that belongs to me," Sheila said. "I want to get it. You wouldn't know if there's a superintendent around, would you? Somebody with a key?"

"You want to get into his flat, eh?" the boy said, a sly look of triumph subtly creeping into his eyes. "There's nobody with a key around here. You'll have to wait."

"No," Sheila exclaimed, and then added more calmly, "I don't have time."

"It's not hard to get in," the boy said offhandedly, "if you know how." Sheila exploded silently. He was playing a cat-and-mouse game with her, forcing her to admit she wanted to get into Bayliss' flat in his absence. All right; she knew his little game and what it meant. She'd play along with him, anything to speed things up. In her dungarees pocket she had thrust some bills before leaving, and now she fingered them. She had a few pound notes, one five-pound note and something better, an American five-dollar bill.

"This is yours," she said, holding the five-dollar bill up, "if you really know what you're talking about." His eyes widened, and a slow smile spread over his grimy face.

"Follow me, mum," he said. "The locks ain't much of anything on these old doors. Besides, nobody what lives around here has anything worth stealin'. And you don't look like the stealin' kind, anyway. I guess you and His Honor had a bit of a falling out, aye?"

He threw her a wink, and Sheila nodded. She didn't care what the little urchin thought. She only wanted to get at the things in that flat. As she followed the boy into the narrow hallway and up the creaking wooden staircase, she felt the musty, dank closeness of the tenement and she shivered. The boy halted before a doorway, took something out of his pocket and worked on the lock for a moment until the door swung open. Sheila handed him the five dollars.

"Is there a back way out of this place?" she questioned. He pointed along the dim hallway to the end, where she saw a doorway at the other end of the corridor.

"The other side of that door, mum; an outside stairway right down to the street."

Sheila watched him saunter back down the stairs and slipped into the room. It was furnished only by two worn chairs and a table. A closet door hung open to one side, and she noted another room beyond as she hurried over to the closet. The clothes hanging there were all work clothes, windbreakers and faded denim trousers, yet she examined each one carefully and thoroughly, unwilling to pass up anything now that she had finally gained admittance to the flat. The adjoining room was a bedroom, and there were more clothes in a closet there: jackets, one suit and various trousers. Again, though, there was nothing to match the button she had found. Beneath the sagging bed she found a suitcase, pulled it out and opened it to see only some dirty shirts. With a kind of desperation, Sheila examined every inch of the flat, even looking into the kitchen cupboards. But it wasn't there; it wasn't any place in the flat. She knew that time was running out; it was getting dangerously late. As she slipped out of that flat, hearing the lock snap shut behind her, she refused to believe that the fruitlessness of her search absolved the man. He could be wearing the jacket she sought, or it could be some place else, at a cleaner's perhaps.

She had just reached the top of the staircase when she saw a figure climbing the steps below her, his big bulk filling the narrow stairway, his black hair rumpled and uncombed.

Dear God, it's him! Sheila groaned to herself. She started to turn to flee when he looked up, his dark eyes burning into her, holding her there.

"You!" he exclaimed, frowning. "What in blazes are you doing around here? You come snoopin' after me?"

His voice had turned into a menacing growl as he slowly mounted the steps, his eyes fixed on her.

"I asked what you are doing here?" he repeated. "You been trying to get into my flat?"

"I came to see you," Sheila said, finding her voice. Bayliss paused for a moment, only a few steps below.

"You've got no cause to come seeing me," he said. "You're up to something."

"No," Sheila lied. "I wanted to see you about that trouble you had with my aunt."

"What for?" the man asked. And then, with the quickness of a snake, his hand shot out and caught Sheila by the wrist, holding her in a grip of iron.

"I heard about what you wanted her to do," Sheila replied. "I like your idea. I want to talk about it. Please, you're hurting my wrist."

The man stood still, turning what she had said over in his mind.

"You like the idea I had?" he said slowly. He opened his heavy fist and let her wrist fall. His feet were on the edge of the top step, balanced precariously, and as he released his grip on her wrist, Sheila acted quickly. With all her strength she threw herself against the man, turning to one side so that her shoulder struck his chest. He roared in anger and surprise as he toppled backwards. She could hear his heavy body crashing down the narrow stairs as she turned and fled for the back entrance. The sound of oaths, mingled with cries of pain told her he had not suffered serious injury, and she leaped down the outside staircase as fast as she could. The stair led to a narrow alleyway between two of the buildings, and Sheila raced for the back of the tenements. She ran along the narrow, cobbled back street, peering down each passageway as she crossed from building to building. If Bayliss hadn't seen the Sunbeam parked at the end of the town, she might be in the clear. Otherwise, she knew he'd be heading for it to cut her off.

She was breathless, her legs hurting, when she reached the car with a sigh of relief. There was no one there, and she threw herself behind the wheel, spun the little auto around and roared away from Multyowen.

In the ride back to Doylan Hall, she wondered more about what she'd tell Brian concerning her escapade than she thought of how narrowly she had missed death. She decided not to tell him until the morning. It was dark when she reached the house, and was suddenly very tired and drained. She turned on the hall light and sank down onto the big sofa in the living room to rest. Sleep overtook her almost instantly, and it was over an hour later when she woke to the sound of the doorbell ringing insistently. At the door, she peered through the narrow panes of glass that flanked each side of the big door. Seeing Brian's figure there, she quickly opened up.

"I fell asleep on the sofa," she explained.

"That's why the house was all dark," he said. "I was worried."

"I checked the hospital on Bridgit," Brian said, following her into the living room. "She's still in a coma, still unconscious. But she's alive."

"I guess we should be grateful for that much," Sheila answered. Brian had sat down beside her on the sofa, and she went into his arms.

"I've something very important to tell you, Brian," the girl said. "It was no accident that injured Bridgit. It was deliberate, and it was intended for me. The lintel had been sawed through at one end so it would fall on me the first time I opened the garage doors to get the car."

Brian's face grew set and tight.

"Are you sure of this?" he asked.

"Absolutely," she answered. "I know a piece of wood that's been sawed from one that has broken off."

"Could the end have been sawed to make repairs, perhaps recently, and then put back?"

"No. From the amount of loose dirt and debris that came down with it, that lintel hasn't been moved since it was put there. No, Brian, it was a clever attempt to create another fatal accident. And it would have worked if Bridgit hadn't needed to run into town for ten minutes."

Sheila leaned back on Brian's arm as it rested over the top of the sofa. As she turned to nestle her head against the sleeve of his jacket, her eyes met the three buttons at the end of the sleeve. Only there weren't three buttons! Sheila stared at the sleeve, at the two buttons and the small, round impression where one was missing. Spellbound, her gaze took in the medium gray of the buttons, flecked with brown markings, distinctive, unmistakable. She sat stone still, her eyes riveted on the two buttons, while a slow coldness seemed to creep up her body, curling around her legs and then over her chest until she felt as though she were being slowly lowered into a pool of icy water. Transfixed by the enormity of what she saw, it was as though she were not really there but an outsider looking in on some terrible, distant event. She felt Brian's hand shaking her shoulder, and she heard his voice suddenly coming of the of the air, like the voice from a radio that has been just turned on.

"Sheila, what is it?" he was saying. "What's the matter?"

"Nothing," the girl said, hearing her own voice as she would that of a stranger. "Why?"

"Because you suddenly seemed to go off into a trance."

Sheila forced her voice to stay even. He was right; she did feel as though she were in a trance.

"I'm not feeling well, that's all," she said. "I guess it's all just catching up with me. I've a terrible headache, and I feel completely washed out. I want to go to bed and sleep for twenty-four hours."

Brian pulled her to her feet, watching her closely, a furrow creasing his brow.

"I think that's a great idea for you," he said. "But I'm concerned over your staying here alone. I think I should stay over in one of the guest rooms."

"No, no," Sheila said, hoping she wasn't sounding too hasty. "I'll be all right, really I will. I can lock my door and the windows. Even if someone got into the house, I'd be safe enough. I just want to be alone, all to myself."

"All right, if you insist," Brian said grudgingly. "But I don't like it much, my girl."

Lord, how could he sound so sincere! Sheila silently asked herself. Even his arm around her as they walked to the door somehow made itself felt through the cold numbness of her body. He smoothed her hair with his hand, brushed her forehead with his lips and hurried off with the plea to call him if she changed her mind. Sheila nodded and slammed the door shut. She pushed over the heavy bolt. The numbness of her body overcame her, and she slid down to lean her head against the polished wood of the big door. She wanted so to call out for him to come back, to show her it was all a nightmare. But all she could see was those two matching buttons and the missing one's imprint. It was a gigantic, monstrous realization that loomed up before her eyes and turned the pit of her stomach into a twisted knot.

She felt alone, lost, betrayed, as she contemplated the ruins of a world now shattered by deceit and disillusion. But even in betrayal, even in deceit there had to be answers, there had to be reasons. There had to be something somewhere that made sense, if only in an evil way. She had to think things through, but first she had to make herself as safe as she could. Pulling herself to her feet, Sheila went from room to room on the main floor, locking each window and trying the rear door until she assured herself she was tightly locked in. Then she climbed the stairs of her own room, locked that stout door and secured the window. Once more a wave of nausea and sickness came over her as she thought of how she had been just about to tell Brian of finding the button and ask him to stay the night. As she undressed, her mind flew back, back to the start, to the new beginning of her return to Connemara. The more she reassembled bits and pieces, the more her heart grew despondent. In vain she sought something to tell her she was wrong, yet everything she examined seemed to fit so neatly.

First, there had been Brian's attempt to make her forget the whole thing by glossing over Aunt Margaret's fears. She was an old, senile woman with an overactive imagination, he had said. Then that terrible night at the Dolmens, he was supposedly away in Dublin. But was he? She never did see her pursuer in the fog and mists of the great Druidic temples. And it was Brian who had made her promise she'd always tell him where she was going. Then wasn't it Brian who had suggested, no, *urged*, that she take the drive this morning to "get away and relax"? He had set up the whole incident, planned it, directed it so it would happen. And it was he who stood to acquire Doylan Hall if she were out of the picture, either by frightening her into rejecting it or by the finality of death. Of course the will had revealed that, but she had never, even in her wildest dreams, connected this with the killings. It was just beyond all belief. And even now it didn't seem enough, not for murder, not for this explosion of hatred.

And she thought of the unexplained things, too, as she cost out in all directions. What of the man Bayliss? Why had Brian tried to convince her Bayliss was not the one? Why not let her think it was Bayliss and keep her from suspecting anyone else? Or were they working together, and had he feared she might get something on Bayliss that would load her to him? It all made up one great, unanswerable and hideous puzzle. *Why, Brian, why?* she hoard herself sob into the loneliness of the looked room. And what of a few nights ago when she was so certain of what his eyes and lips had said, the unspoken words of a love that had never died'? Or was it something else that had never died? *I'm not the forgetting kind.* Those were the words he had said to her, and now, as she heard them again in her mind, she realized they could have an ominous ring to them.

Seven years ago they had parted with such terrible bitterness and anger. Could a man harbor such hatred for so many years? She know the answer was yes. Others had done it for longer times, and the history of human relationships was replete with undying hatreds. Was that what he was net forgetting: the hatred, the feeling of being a fool before all his friends in Duncavan as she had run off and left him? Years of brooding and hating and turning in on oneself could warp the mind and twist the emotions. It had happened before to others. Love and hate were so very close, anyway, it took little to slip from one into the other. And so the questions came one after the other, tumbling like leaves in a fall wind, over and over without pause, without pattern. But one thing did emerge with terrible clarity. Instead of gathering happiness and friendship and warmth here in Connemara, she found herself surrounded by fear and solitude and cold death. And most of all, instead of love, she had found hate.

Yet again and again like a sweet chord in a disharmonious symphony, the taste of Brian's lips kept returning. It was as if they were carrying a message of their own, a message which said this is real, this is more than can be ignored. Or was it nothing but her own desperate wish she was hearing? The button in the pocket of her dungarees was real, too, too real and too demanding to turn away from. There was no time left to look the other way, and there was no turning back, either. She had to go on, as fast as she could, for she was in a race with death. She did not want to go to sleep, but weariness and shock finally overtook the frightened but determined girl, and she fell into a deep slumber.

CHAPTER EIGHT

Morning came. Sheila woke, still alive, and knelt beside the bed in a prayer of gratitude. She dressed hurriedly, fixed a small breakfast and phoned Tom Grogan in Duncavan. She wanted him to come at once to open the old, safe, but the man was adamant. He was finishing a job he had started yesterda, and it would be late afternoon before he could come. There was nothing to do but wait, and Sheila decided to wait inside Doylan Hall, on the theory that a prisoner can be safest inside his prison. Brian called early, and she put him off without arousing his susicions, she fearfully hoped. She made two calls of her own, first to the hospital to inquire about Bridgit. The woman's condition remained unchanged, hanging in that dim world between life and death. The second call was to Harry Glendon, and at once the soft, quiet unruffled calm of his voice was a soothing comfort to the churning of her heart.

"I'm going to try to get to your place tonight," Sheila told him. "If I don't appear by nine-thirty, please call Constable Connaughten and tell him to go to Doylan Hill."

"Of course, my dear," the voice said. "But you sound distraught. Perhaps I should come to see you."

"No, no," Sheila said quickly, her voice rising in alarm. Harry Glendon was her one remaining hope for help. She couldn't risk his life, for his sake or for the sake of her own plans. Someone would no doubt be watching the house tonight, perhaps even now. Bayliss, probably, if he and Brian were working together.

Terence's disappearance was too chillingly fresh in her memory. It could happen to Harry Glendon, and then she would be truly alone. They had gone too far to stop at one more killing. Sheila thought of going to Constable Connaughten with the button and her story, but she realized it would not be enough. It was open to too many easy explanations. Brian, after all, was a respected solicitor in Duncavan and undoubtedly fairly well acquainted with the constable. No, she needed a tighter case. She needed to find out that key to it all which Aunt Margaret had uncovered. She needed more time, and she was bargaining for that time with her life.

Meanwhile, she had decided that it would pose no greater risk to go to Harry Glendon's by the dark of the night. The night was made for crime, and death would be there, waiting for her, trying to find her again. But the dark could be made an ally, just as she had made the fog and the Dolmens an ally that night. Sheila knew the moors as well, perhaps a good deal better, than anyone. And so it was a risk she would take. Once more she would face death in the darkness, but this time, despite her fear, her shock and her inner pain, a certain grim determination had settled upon the girl. She found herself excited in anticipation when Tom Grogan finally arrived and began to pry open the heavy door of the old safe in the study. The iron box resisted strongly and staunchly but finally gave way, and the door swung open in defeat. When Tom Grogan left, Sheila hurriedly scooped out of the contents of the safe. Some old property deeds and unimportant memoranda came first, then an old lapel watch and some random pieces of old documents, plus a metal lock-box. It was the lock-box that held three strange and curious items.

The first was a bronze medallion Sheila picked up in her hand, engraved with a leaping dolphin on the face side and an inscription on the reverse. As she read the inscription, she became convinced that these three pieces were important to the puzzle she was trying to solve. They concerned no one Sheila had ever heard Aunt Margaret mention and they were cryptic in themselves, but most important, Aunt Margaret had secreted them in the safe. Sheila frowned, searching her own memory, as she read the inscription on the bronze medallion:

> Leila Stowft
> Free-stroke Champion
> St. Agnes — 1949

Who was Leila Stowft? Sheila pondered. Why was she important, important enough for Aunt Margaret to have an old medallion she had won hidden in the safe? Sheila picked up the next item, a letter to her aunt, and read it aloud to herself:

Lady Margaret Doylan
Doylan Hall
Duncavan, Connemara
Dear Lady Margaret:

 As per your inquiry, our records show that Miss Leila Stowft was a student here at St. Agnes School and did indeed win the free-stroke swimming championship in 1949. She resided then at 226 Wexford Street, Dublin.

Sister Mary Josephine
Department of Records,
St. Agnes' School

Obviously, Aunt Margaret had written to find out the truth of the inscription on the medallion. But why? Why had she ever questioned the validity of the inscription? The last item was a slip of paper bearing the words: *British Soldiers—Center Section.*

Sheila pondered the meaning of the words scrawled on the slip of paper. Her aunt had put these things away for safekeeping because they supplied the key parts of the puzzle, she was certain of that, and now that she had the parts she had to find how they fitted together. An inner sense told her she was near the answers she sought. If she could remain alive she would have Aunt Margaret's killer. Sheila felt a sense of irony, to be so close to the truth and so close to death at the same time.

There was ample food in the house, and Sheila forced herself to eat as night descended over the land. Outside the tightly closed windows she could hear a nightingale sing, and the sweet loveliness of its song was a silver dagger piercing her heart. Brian had called at least four times during the day, his voice ringing with concern, and each time she had turned aside his offers to come out. And each time when she put down the phone, she could not see for the tears in her eyes. How utterly and ridiculously stupid, she told herself, to be in love with a man who wanted to kill you. But then, she had come to realize, even horror cannot put out a flame which has burned for so long a time.

Angrily, Sheila pushed aside all thoughts of betrayal and hurt and despair. There was no time for that now. There was time only to concentrate on the immediate task ahead, to get to Harry Glendon and put everything before him. Perhaps he could supply the answers to make the pieces fit. She took a tote bag she had brought from America and carefully stuffed the two old newspapers, the medallion and the other items of the lock-box into it. The button she let stay in the pocket of her dungarees. It was too small and too easy to lose, and she could tell him about it easily enough. She rested a sweater on top of everything to prevent them from falling out and to keep them hidden, as well. She tied the drawstring of the tote bag securely, slung it over her shoulder and then turned on the two big lamps in the living room and the light in her room. She went over to the window so the watching eyes she could feel out there in the dark would see her.

It was a *dubh* night, a black night with no moon showing. That was good. Once she got to the moors, she would be relatively safe. The ever-present fog would be her cloak there, and she was confident she could lose any pursuer on that wild and shrouded stretch of land. In fact, and she could not conceal a grim satisfaction, the killer could have a fatal accident that would actually be an accident. It was getting out of the house and to the moors that would present the greatest problem. She strolled over to the window again, lifted her arms and pulled her dress over her head. Then she slowly moved away from the window. Once out of sight of anyone watching outside, she hurriedly donned slacks and a heavy dark blue sweater, slung the tote bag over her other shoulder to free her right arm, and slipped out of the room. She hurried along a corridor to where a narrow doorway stood at the far end, close beside the kitchen entrance. Opening it, she switched on the flashlight she had picked up from the nail where it hung beside the kitchen door. The flight of wooden steps to the cellar brought back memories of all the times she had trod them as a little girl. Her light, moving eerily before her, picked out the old wine kegs, cobwebby and dusty, the seldom used tool rack and the wheelbarrow.

It seemed only yesterday she had played in this musty old cellar. She moved the light slowly along the stone walls and the thick crossbeams until she found what she was seeking, a small set of stone steps that led up to a pair of wooden doors that opened onto the yard at the side of the house. Flat, flush to the ground, the doors opened upward and were once used to roll the big wine kegs in and out of the cellar. Two heavy iron bolts secured them, but after a few minutes the girl managed to free them from their shell of rust and slowly, carefully, taking care to avoid squeaking hinges, pushed them open. She was counting on her guess that if two were watching the house, one would be posted at the front door and the other at the back. She closed the cellar doors and, staying in a low crouch, waited to listen for any sound in the night. But the loudest noise she heard was the pounding of her heart. A row of rhododendron bushes extended some thirty feet from the corner of the house and, staying in a crouch, she scurried over to them, moving alongside their dark shape until she neared the moors. The fog that immediately began to envelop her had never been more welcome. It was a deadly game she was playing, but she had decided to play it to the hilt. Once on the moors, she made for the edge of the cliffs, using her knowledge of the wind's sweep and sea's noise to follow the line of the cliffs with a desperate sureness that surprised even herself.

When at last she saw the row of dark hedges loom up ahead, she knew Harry Glendon's cottage had to be but a short way beyond. Then she saw the small circle of light glowing through the fog. Moments later she was inside the warmth of the thatched roof cottage, and Harry Glendon was guiding her to a soft, covered chair by the fireplace.

"Now you just relax and get your breath, young lady," he said in his gentle manner. "I'm sure we can work this all out tonight, but before we go into it, I've been doing a lot of thinking, and I feel there are some things I must bring up."

The older man settled himself in a chair opposite Sheila and looked at her quietly, reassuringly.

"You are still a very young girl," he said. "Have you thought about forgetting all this ugliness and returning to America? You know, people have spent a lifetime in search for something which constantly eluded them. You are too lovely and young to spend your life in bitterness and doubt. Now, I don't mean to tell you what to do but only to think about it. What really happened to

Lady Margaret may be so buried in conflicting evidence that no amount of searching could turn up the kind of clear-cut proof that the authorities would need.

"Perhaps if you went back to America for a few years, perhaps only for a year, you could come back again with a different approach to it all. Your narrow escapes, your fears and apprehensions would be put aside by the passage of time."

Sheila was grateful for the understanding that seemed to lie just behind those dark eyes. His words seemed to come from that deep pain he carried some place within him.

"I appreciate what you're saying," Sheila said. "Really I do. But I can't stop, not now. You see, I think I'm very close to it. A lot happened yesterday; a lot of terrible and frightening things have come to light."

"All right, my dear," Harry Glendon said, settling back in his chair. "Suppose you tell me all that you've found out."

Her words tumbling forth, Sheila started by recounting how she had found the garage door lintel sawed through and then about the button on the floor. When she told him of finding it was from Brian's jacket, she could not stop the tears that flooded her eyes. Angrily, she wiped them away.

"I'm sorry," she apologized. "I guess I haven't recovered from it yet. It was so completely unexpected, and it hurt so deeply."

The older man shook his head sadly.

"What a terrible discovery indeed," he murmured. "The world is often a cruel and shocking place. That's what Leila always used to say. Leila was my first wife, God rest her soul."

Leila! The name exploded in Sheila's mind like a skyrocket. *Leila! Leila Stowft!* That was the name on the back of the medallion and in the letter to Aunt Margaret from St. Agnes' School. And that Leila was a swimming champion with a medallion to show for it, while Harry Glendon's first wife, *his* Leila had

drowned in a boating accident because she *couldn't swim.* Could
the Leila of the medallion and the letter be the same person as
Leila Glendon? Was Harry Glendon's wife the same one as the
championship swimmer? If so, the dark thoughts that swept over
Sheila were too hideous to consider. She looked at the sad, lined
face of the man seated opposite her and those deep, unfathomable
eyes. My, God, she inwardly cried, is there no place to turn? Is
there no trust anywhere, no balm in Gilead? Am I surrounded by
evil? What has happened to this lovely hamlet? Aunt Margaret's
words to her had been that there was something monstrously
evil here in Duncavan. Had she been referring to some terrible,
creeping poison which had infested all of Duncavan? Sheila felt
as though she were caught up in a gigantic whirlpool, being
swirled and tossed and buffeted and completely helpless.

She had to get away from there. The little cottage and the
sad-eyed man were also drenched in evil. There was no trust to
be found here, not now, not until she knew more. She got to her
feet abruptly, too abruptly.

"What is it?" Harry Glendon asked. "You've suddenly become
so pale and tense. What's the matter?"

"I'm feeling sick," Sheila answered, and it was not a lie. "It's
my stomach, all this tension and nervousness. I can't think about
it any more tonight. I must go back and lie down."

"But you've just come," the man protested, getting to his feet.
"Isn't there a lot more you wanted to tell me?"

"No, not really," Sheila said, hearing the shakiness of her
voice. "I just had to tell someone about finding the button.
And I will consider everything you brought up, I promise. It's
been a long day, a hard day, and I've just go to get back and
lie down."

"Then let me take you back to Doylan Hall at least," Harry
Glendon offered.

"No, please!" Sheila exclaimed, immediately angry at herself for having declined too sharply, too quickly. "We could both be in danger then. I can make it better alone. I'll phone you when I'm home safely. All right?"

"Whatever you wish, my dear," the man said gently. He patted Sheila's shoulder as he opened the door for her. "Don't worry. Everything will work out, you'll see."

Grateful again for the dark and the fog, Sheila breathed a sigh of relief as she started back across the moors. He had sounded so sympathetic, so understanding, just as Brian had sounded so concerned. Was everyone in Duncavan a consummate actor, or was she too caught up in the whole ugly business to see clearly? Were they all in it together in some monstrous plot? Or, and it was just as possible, was each trying to get rid of her for his own reasons? She caught herself up sharply. It would do no good to go on in wild speculation. There was a key, an answer, and it lay among the things inside the tote bag over her shoulder. Once she found it, she would know some of the facts at least, and the rest would surely fall into place in time.

The fog was heavy now as she crossed the moors, and she used her flashlight to help pick out her way. No one would be able to lie in wait here in this denseness, but she would have to be careful when she neared the house. As she watched the beam of her flashlight fight its way through the fog, lighting patches of ground wherever it could find a wispy opening, she estimated she was halfway across the moors when the light fell upon the spot of red. She let the light travel across the thin line of red-tipped lichen growing out of the soil, rising up about an inch from the ground. Their red tips in a symmetrical row recalled how Aunt Margaret had first shown them to her as a child. Their red crests, row after row, reminiscent of the red coats of British Grenadiers on parade, had given them their common name of

British Soldiers. Sheila stopped still as the words flashed across her mind, scrawled on the slip of paper from the safe … *British Soldiers!* How did these red-crested, fruiticose lichens figure in the mystery? But they must, somehow. That was why Aunt Margaret had cryptically written their name and put it with the other evidence. Half-running again, Sheila knew she was getting wonderfully and perilously near to the answers. She had to get back into Doylan Hall safely, to spread everything she had out before her, to do what she had intended to do with Harry Glendon: unlock the puzzle once and for all.

She switched off the flashlight as she drew nearer to the house and went the rest of the way on silent, catlike feet. As she came within sight of Doylan Hall, she saw the light in the window of her room still burning brightly and the lesser glow from the living room windows. The fog was now reaching to the house itself, but the girl took no chances, dropping down to crouch low along the dark protection of the rhododendron hedges. Once more she felt eyes in the night, eyes watching the house, watching for her. She scooted from the hedges to the cellar doors and into the basement. Bolting the doors after her, she stood quietly, hearing the harsh sound of her own breathing, listening for footsteps inside the house. But if anyone had entered he was waiting silently. It was a risk she'd have to take, and as she went upstairs she paused to examine both the back and the front doors. Both were untouched and, taking a deep breath of relief, she went into the living room and emptied the contents of the tote bag on the large oval table.

CHAPTER NINE

Sheila looked at the objects laid out before her: the bronze medallion, the letter, the slip of paper and the two old newspapers. Only the button was missing, and that was a part of the mystery she already knew about, to her bitter despair. Sheila picked up the older of the two newspapers, and this time she had something to look for, the name Leila Stowft. Perhaps there was an account of the tragedy in the journal. But it was not an account of the "accident" she found. It was an item in the wedding section that now leaped out at her as if it tried to say it had been waiting to be discovered.

LEILA STOWFT MARRIES MR. HARRY GLENDON read the caption, and now Sheila knew why Aunt Margaret had sent away for the journal and why she had requested the information from St. Agnes'. "Miss Leila Stowft of 226 Wexford Street, Dublin," the social item said. Sheila turned the bronze medallion over in her hand as the horrible truth of it began to dawn upon her as it must have dawned upon Aunt Margaret. She began to envision the scene as Aunt Margaret must have realized the truth. Somehow her aunt had come upon the medallion and, knowing that the mere overturning of a rowboat would not cause a championship swimmer to drown, had decided to investigate further. True to her character, she would not accuse, or allow herself to conclude anything without unimpeachable proof. She had written to St. Agnes' for verification of the medal and the girl named Leila Stowft of 226 Wexford Street. Then a request for back issues of the newspaper clenched the truth of her suspicions. Leila Stowft and Leila Glendon were indeed one and the same person, and the rowboat "accident" had been no accident at all but murder.

Now Sheila turned to the second newspaper and opened it to the wedding section at once. Once more the name Harry Glendon stared back at her, a smaller, less conspicuous item this time, but nonetheless there. The announcement described the wedding of one Mrs. Charlotte Ryder to Mr. Harry Glendon of Duncaven, and it described the bride as a woman of some inherited wealth. It was clear, all too clear at last. If the first "accident" had been proven murder to Aunt Margaret's satisfaction, then she suspected the death of the second Mrs. Glendon at the foot of the cliffs was no more of an "accident." Sheila recalled one line of Lady Margaret's last letter as it leaped out at her with sickening clarity ... "I'm afraid I have blundered in this unfamiliar role. Please hurry and come."

Somehow, Aunt Margaret had let Harry Glendon discover she had become suspicious, and he had succeeded in making her death a part of the same monstrous series of tragic "accidents." Impulsively, Sheila turned to call Brian but halted before the phone. No, that was impossible. Somewhere he fitted into the picture. Perhaps he and Glendon were the real conspirators and Bayliss only their hired hand. The infinite sadness came over her again as she thought of Brian as a part of all this, and in a real way she was now sorry she had returned to Connemara. If she had stayed in New York she could have always had the dream, the magic, comforting dream of what might have been. It would have been incomplete, but better than the unbearable pain she felt at present.

The small slip of paper with the words scrawled on it—*British Soldiers—Center Section*—was all that remained to fit in, and she knew it had to fit in some place. She took up her flashlight. She had to go back on the moors and complete the picture. So once more she retraced her path out the cellar doors and back upon the fogbound moors. She didn't switch on the light until she was far onto the wild land, for she had the distinct feeling she was being followed this time. Crossing back and forth in the fog, she tried to elude her pursuer, if there really was someone pursuing her. When she snapped on the flash, she followed its hesitant beam until she saw them suddenly appear, the red-tipped lichens growing in a long, thin line across the ground, one after the other in a neat row, miniature British Soldiers indeed. With the flashlight, she followed the line to its end, then doubled back to the other end and retraced her steps until she found the center of the long, thin line. There, the girl knelt down on the soft dampness of the earth and examined the ground closely, shining the light along the edges of the tiny branched stalks. A neat, thin crack in the surface of the soil, no more than a slight indented ridge of dirt, ran alongside the lichens for about two feet. Leaning over to the other side of the red-crest lichens, she saw an identical thin indentation. Using her fingers, she found that a section of the ground lifted out easily, the red-tipped plants standing atop it like candles on a birthday cake. Sheila lifted the entire section loose and laid it to one side as she stared down at a narrow metal box buried in the ground. She reached down and opened the cover of the box to reveal a cache of jeweled clips, brooches, pins and necklaces, that, even in the fog, managed to glitter.

She was sitting there, staring at her find, when the voice came at her from the darkness, a soft and gentle voice.

"It's too bad, my dear," the voice said, and, looking up, Sheila saw the tall thin frame of Harry Glendon take shape in the fog. "You had to continue to snoop. You and your aunt are too much alike for your own good."

Sheila was held by the eyes again, deeper and sadder with a hollowness behind them that defied penetration. And now she realized something else, that the pain and grief in them was not from what she imagined but the pain of a tortured soul, the grief of a twisted mind.

"It's all true, then," Sheila said. "You killed Aunt Margaret because she found out your first wife had been murdered, not drowned in an accident, and she suspected you killed your second wife also."

"Yes," the man admitted, taking a step nearer to the girl. "Not that you'll be telling anyone!"

"Why did you do it? Kill your two wives, I mean," Sheila asked and instantly knew that her question could not be answered in simple terms. Here was no robber, no ordinary killer, no rapist, no one who killed out of anger. Here was a psychopath, a sickness that walked as a man.

"It saddens me to kill," he said, as if reading her thoughts. "It really does, you know. But then, killing is necessary in this world, as necessary as sleeping and eating. Nature doesn't frown on killing; she recognizes the necessity of killing. Nature uses one form of life to supply nourishment and sustenance to another. It is in her scheme of things that killing accomplishes this. Neither of my wives were beautiful or productive. They were really quite useless to society. By their deaths, their lives took on value. It gave meaning to their drab existences, just as the queen bee gives meaning to the life of the drone. By their deaths, they made it possible for me to exist more fully. That is not contrary to but in accord with nature's ways. Your aunt of course was different, a snooping old woman who would have upset the delicate balance of my existence. So you see, contrary to what man likes to believe, killing is an important part of living."

Glendon stepped closer, and Sheila shrank back, aware that there was no place to hide out there in the moors.

"You could have avoided all this by minding your own business," he said, his voice taking on a hard edge. "But it's too late to think about that now. When you left so suddenly after I made the error of mentioning Leila's name, I knew what had happened, that you had found the medallion. I never know what had become of the medallion after Lady Margaret found it near here on one of her morning walks. I'd carelessly dropped it, and as she asked me about it I could see suspicions forming in her mind. I should have thrown the medallion away long ago. It wasn't worth anything. I guess I'm just a sentimentalist at heart."

"You're a monster," Sheila flared back. "A demented, sick monster."

"You refuse to understand, too." Harry Glendon sighed, wearily, as though it saddened him to realize so few people understood truth. "After Lady Margaret's suspicions began to take shape, I had to act. I couldn't sit by and let her amass enough evidence to put me in jail, now could I? You see, both my wives had considerable expensive jewelry, certainly enough to keep a modest man such as myself living comfortably. I also collect from insurance policies I had the foresight to take out on both of those good women. Now it wouldn't look right for someone, perhaps just a cleaning woman, to find all this substantial jewelry lying about my little cottage, particularly when I declared myself destitute and penniless upon their deaths. This way I also collect a small stipend from the government. With the jewelry safely hidden out here on the moors, it's unable to cause me any embarrassment. I make a trip to Dublin or London every two or three months to sell one of the pieces. It was all working out so nicely until I dropped that medallion and your aunt found it."

"Terence," Sheila said. "You killed Terence, too, then."

"A simple precaution." Harry Glendon smiled, and the girl shivered. "I didn't know how much your aunt had confided in him. I couldn't risk you learning what he might be able to tell you. And of course your cook, poor soul … you correctly figured out that the lintel was designed to strike you. Your luck has been fantastic, first at the Dolmens and then with the garage doors. But it has run out, my dear."

"Not quite yet." Another voice cut through the fog, and Sheila whirled to see the sturdy, square figure of Brian emerge from the swirling mists. "It's you who have run out of luck, Glendon."

Sheila's heart spun as she saw Brian with a mixture of relief and hope and astonishment. She wanted to run into his arms, to cling there and let her terror-stricken body draw new strength from his touch. But as she turned, she was suddenly held in a vise-like grip as hands seized her arms to yank her backwards. Then Harry Glendon's one arm was around her throat, and she saw the glint of the knife held against her breast.

"No," he said hoarsely, "I'm not through being lucky. I've just acquired this lovely insurance policy."

"Let go of that girl," Brian commanded as he moved forward. Harry Glendon's answer was to push the point of the knife forward, and Sheila gasped in pain as the blade went into her breast, just deeply enough to draw blood.

"One step more and it'll go into her heart," the man warned. Brian stood still, and Sheila saw the mists close in around his figure as she was dragged backwards.

"You are going to have another accident, just like the one your aunt had," Harry Glendon said in her ear, and uncompromising savagery in his voice now. "Then I'll take care of your friend."

Sheila heard the roar of the waves pounding the shore as it was borne up by the sweeping wind that scaled the cliffs. They were near the edge, nearer than she had thought.

"No," she gasped, "no!" But the arm around her neck only tightened as she helplessly clawed at it. She wanted to scream, but she was barely able to breathe. He was going to choke her into unconsciousness before sending her hurtling off the edge of the cliffs. Another kind of darkness was descending upon her when a figure shot out of the fog and she felt herself being flung forward to the ground, along with Harry Glendon. The arm around her throat lifted, and Sheila wrenched herself free, rolling to one side to see Brian getting to his feet. He had circled around them in the fog, she saw, to wait at the very edge of the cliffs and then tackle them both. But Harry Glendon still had the long-bladed knife, and she saw his tall, spare figure charge Brian with the weapon.

Brian met the charge from a crouch, and both men seemed almost to rise up into the air as they grappled together. Brian twisted his body, and Sheila saw the killer catapult into the air to land with a thud at the very edge of the cliff. Brian was after him at once, but the man had the maniacal strength of the insane and the desperation of a killer. He flung the younger man back as one would fling a sack of wheat, and Sheila screamed as she saw him charge forward with the knife upraised. He dived at Brian, and in the swirl of the fog Sheila could see Brian rolling over on the ground to try to avoid the plunging blade. The fog enveloped them in its opaque shield, and the girl could hear more than she could see. Fists clenched until they dug into the palms of her hand, Sheila saw the shadowy shapes as they tumbled and rolled and struggled, barely visible for a moment and then swallowed up by the fog, only to emerge 'again for another instant.

She heard a sharp cry, Brian's voice, and heart stopped. And then, cutting through the night like the wail of a banshee, she heard a scream of terror. It pierced the air and trailed waveringly away until it was but an echo and only the sound of the sea below was heard. A figure, like an out of focus picture, moved toward the girl in the fog. She watched, waiting, transfixed. If she had wanted to turn and run, she could not have managed. Besides, there was no more place left for running. Slowly, like a curtain parting, the mists moved aside to reveal Brian standing there, his left arm stained with red.

Her knees felt weak, but she made them run as she rushed into his arms.

"It's done with, Sheila McCloud," he murmured. "It's done with."

"You're hurt, my darling," she sobbed. "You're hurt."

"Nothing that won't neal," he said. "He had the strength of a dozen men. His knife caught my arm as he flew over me and over the cliff. Come; let's get you home."

"It's better this way," Brian said later as Sheila wrapped the bandage around his upper arm. His jacket, the jacket, hung over the chair, and he sat with his shirt off while she finished dressing the wound. "It's over and done."

"I knew something was wrong when you changed so suddenly last night," he told her. "I wanted to shake you, to come here and make you tell me what it was. But I knew better. You're so confounded stubborn, Sheila McCloud. Why were you suddenly so afraid of me?"

When Sheila told him about finding the button from his jacket at the garage, the fear still inside her leaped forward again. Nothing that had happened this night had explained away that terrible discovery.

"So that was it." Brian smiled ruefully. "Yes, I did go to the garage, but after I left you at the door. I decided to check the car myself again, and I remember catching my sleeve on the door when I left. I hadn't even noticed the button was missing.

Glendon stole into the garage and sawed the end of the beam sometime later that night."

Brian pulled the girl down on his lap and her lips onto his. He let his hand gently move through her black hair, his touch soothing on her head.

"I suppose I can't blame you for running in the other direction," he said. "It was incriminating, and you didn't really know anything much about how I felt except that I had doubted your story when you first brought it up. That's why I decided not to press you but to stick close and wait to see what you were going to do."

Sheila shuddered in Brian's arms.

"I'm so glad you did," she said. "What if you hadn't? I'd be dead now, at the bottom of the cliffs."

"You almost outfoxed me," Brian admitted. "You would have anyone else watching the house. But then I remembered the cellar doors. You forget that we used to play there as children. I guessed you wouldn't be walking out the front door as if you were going shopping, and the rear door was too easy a second choice. That's when I thought of the old cellar entrance. Now aren't you glad I've a good memory?"

"Yes." Sheila nodded and buried her head in his arms. "I'm glad you're not the forgetting kind."

Brian's lips were upon hers again, and this time there was no mistaking their message. He had not forgotten, just as she had never been able to forget, and at his touch she felt warm and alive and at peace once again.

"I've come home," she whispered. "We can start again, Brian. We've both learned and lived, and we can make up for lost time. We'll make Doylan Hall into a happy house again, Brian. We'll fill it with laughter and music and the sounds of happiness."

Brian's arms tightened around her. "Aye, we'll do that and more," he replied, and Sheila knew that Aunt Margaret was smiling now. "One more thing," Brian added. "I called the hospital late this afternoon. Bridgit has come out of the coma. She's going to be all right."

Sheila relaxed in the happy circle of his arms and sighed contentedly as the blue-gray light of dawn tinted the sky. The day would be *fine* indeed.

www.ingramcontent.com/pod-product-compliance
Lightning Source LLC
Chambersburg PA
CBHW030350180626
46812CB00007B/2834